I0831229

Chapter 1

Ring Around the Moon

You could say Richard Michaels had a time machine in his kitchen.

On one perfectly gorgeous day, he took notice of a cramped stuffed drawer that needed emptying. It was a characterless drawer in appearance. One you can find anywhere. Just about, anybody could fess up to possessing such a simple thing in his or her house or in his or her kitchen. A space for providing a home away from home for items that have lost their way such as pens that have lost their ink or fasteners that have lost what they once held. A place where things appear to grow in secret mostly unnoticed until we come upon them again. It is at that time, and in such a space, the unexpected sight of an item can betray the membrane shell that keeps out a long since forgotten emotion and gives up a hidden ghost messing about between the strands of a lost memory.

In between one space and beginning in another, Richard saved his drawer for last. Every time he moved from one home to another, he moved the contents of this drawer with him with a purpose only he may one day hope to know. There was not a thing in the drawer that would make anyone else linger or stop anyone from throwing out the objects in the simple drawer. To us, it would be just a cluttered pack rat's drawer, but to Richard it was personal.

The contents were photographs, Christmas cards, Valentine's Day cards, unredeemed gift cards, small change, and loose beads from a broken neckband and deserted key chains; he had accumulated in prior drawers from previous doors, safety locks, and motor vehicles that he once possessed lifetimes ago. Richard did not consciously connect to the physical object he picked up, but dissociated a sinking sensation of alienation he experienced to an awful night's sleep.

The Sun They Called the Moon`

The oldest keys were some of the last items in the drawer. Just a few stone beads left of green quartz and turquoise. The beads were loose and separate from a trio of beads on three strands of waxed brown linen. Richard's fingers bobbed numerously back and forth grasping autonomously between the pairs of knots on the three strands of waxed brown linen. At the moment it took one of the beads to fall and slide across the wooden floor, he removed the keys from the broken pendants and charms then prototypically laid them out in order.

Richard gave little mind to most of the keys knowing that they would never open any door again, but there was one key he no longer remembered. Too tarnished to be anything but old and holding too stubborn an impression over him to let it go. Belatedly, Richard slowly began to recall the space the key once opened.

Chapter 2

Child of the Moon

I lay on my old bed in a new room of our new house and with my hands locked under my head; I stared into the emptiness of the ceiling. I had first lived with my parents at my grandmother's enormous two-story house. I felt a wistful affection for the home and thought of the Rizzos who used to live next door to us on the hill. I remembered Mr. Rizzo as being a heavyset man with a barrel for a belly and a stone for a nose, short in height and low on wit. He was most partial to a dirty old straw hat that covered his bald spot. He usually wore a sleeveless undershirt, and if the wind was blowing from his direction, it carried a smell as if the one cloth had one time been misused to make cheese. What I remembered of his wife was her uncanny gift for ugliness. She too carried her own strange aromatic blend with her like a cloud of foul gas.

The Sun They Called the Moon`

I was about six years old; I recall walking on spring's first soft grass, and crawling through the burrow, I had constructed in my grandmother's Pheasant Berry and Himalayan honeysuckle hedges that bound the two yards. It was a huge living green sculptured wall. It rustled against the cool spring air. The hedges provided some birds a sanctuary but not from a six-year-old, their nervously chirping beaks filling the blue-sky with sounds over my head as I crawled under and through it. The hedges tiny green leafs, breathing with every breeze above me trembling by my very crawl through a living wall, I went back to pick up my red baseball cap and then I went to ask Rizzo why he was digging a hole in the middle of his yard.

"Hey, Mr. Rizzo Why are you digging such a neat hole for?"

"Hay is for-the horse," Rizzo said, as the sweat poured down on his dirt-stained once white tee shirt.

"What did you say, Mr. Rizzo?"

"I say, Hay is for-the horse, what's a matta...you deaf, or something?" Rizzo dug deeper and faster.

I looked on with a meddling desire to learn of his great secret and understand, and asked him, "But Mr. Rizzo, why are you digging' such a neat hole in your yard?"

"How come you no in school this morning, huh?" Rizzo said as he continued dumping a bunch of dirt with his shovel.

"My mom said I didn't have to go today. How come you're not working today, Mr. Rizzo?" I asked.

"How come-a you father and you uncles not a work, how come-a everybody's family stay home together today and watch the tele visionary and listen to the radio? Because everybody in the world gone crazy, that's-a why."

"So you're going crazy too?" I asked.

"I no have gone crazy. I have gone a smart," said Rizzo pointing to the temple of his head and standing to attention in his hole with a reassuring grin.

"Don't you have a tele visionary, Mr. Rizzo? Is that why you're digging a hole because you don't have a tele visionary?" I said with my eyes opening wide-eyed waiting for the answer, standing above him.

"I have-the tele visionary. But I-a no watch," replied Rizzo going back to his digging.

"But why are you digging a hole for?" I said. Mr. Rizzo dug harder and faster. "I bet if you keep digging you're gonna hit China dirt, Mr. Rizzo." Rizzo stopped digging and looked up at me from his hole in the ground.

"I digga the hole because I digga the hole," said Rizzo turning the dirt over, "If I'm-a no lucky, China come here, if I'm-a lucky."

"Huh?" I said.

"Billy," I heard my mother call from the window.

"Do I have to mom; can't I stay?" I said looking towards the window.

"No, I want you to come in," she replied. She sounded like she meant it.

"Listen to you mama. She's-a calling you," said Rizzo as he dumped another pile of dirt.

"Goodbye, Mr. Rizzo," I said.

"Bye-bye, Billy," I heard him say. I was crawling back under and through another of my undercover spaces this time through the

The Sun They Called the Moon`

Japanese Andromeda shrubs with their glossy leaves and drooping clusters of white flowers, and then I continued on my hands and knees under the firethorns. I ran through the back yard, past the porch, stopped to pick up my baseball cap that flew off my head and continued to race around the side of the low vegetation, taking the corner and opening the door, running up the stairs and out of breath.

"Do I gotta come in?" I asked.

"There is no such word as "gotta," my mother replied as she leaned over and picked me up. "There is enough broken English around here. I am not going to let my son run around as if he just got off a banana boat!" I laughed, after all, a banana boat.... She hugged me laughing with me.

Chapter 3

Moon of Agony

Susan was a stay at home mom who never wore curlers and committed herself never to do so. It was part of her choice to herself, "to never let herself go." No commitment was needed, never was she lazy with her appearance or anything else for that matter, sometimes to the point of stubbornness. Susan took a long look at me and pulled my red baseball cap over my eyes. I straightened it.

Susan was one of the fireside "chat" children of the late 1930's and early 1940's, known as the Fireside Chats, a series of thirty evening radio addresses given by the United States President Franklin D. Roosevelt. As if the radio chats, was a conversation that could ever be more than a one-way conversation. However, for a child growing up in the 1940's, chat with an adult was usually one-way on the receiving end. Notwithstanding, they were enormously successful and attracted more listeners than the most popular radio shows during the "Golden Age of Radio."

In the year 1933, there came power, rising like a hand of darkness upon the world. A small faction of ambitious and unscrupulous men organized and found the truths, which were self-evident to Thomas Jefferson, which has been obvious to many generations of Americans, which have influenced the thinking of human rights in the core principles of freedom of man and freedom of mind were to these men, hateful.

Therefore, sitting by the radio, she eavesdropped to why her father was fighting faraway at war. The Fireside Chats were a periodic family function with a personal stake that she could feel personally.

The agenda of a small camarilla of determined and unscrupulous politicos who were happy to sell their country in order to gain power, men focused to cancel forever the propositions of the rights of the will of the people, declaring that the individual person is not entitled to himself and no right by virtue of his collective humanity. That the individual human being has no right to a personal God of his own, a thought of his own, a spoken or written word of his own, or a business of his own; or even to live where he or she pleases or to marry who he or she loves. His only duty is the duty of obedience, not to his God, not to his conscience, but to the will of the few.

The church, as they conceived it, was a monstrosity to be destroyed by every means for corresponding to their agenda, the only one church, it is to be a "World Church," a pagan church, entirely, and exclusively in the service of but one doctrine, one race, one world. The free, self-governing persons were an impossible and an incomprehensible conception to them. Likewise, the government to this small faction of ambitious and unscrupulous men was not to be the servant, but the instrument for the absolute masters and dictators to impose their will on the people, on every act, and to cover-up, their inhuman acts against them.

Susan's generation had been a generation called on to answer and to flush out an old world order hiding in disguise as new world doctrines, again. They were the doctrines to absolute obedience to rule by the few and fortunate, of the suppression of truth, of the oppression of conscience, which free people have long ago rejected.

What Susan's generation faced, therefore, was straightforward and uncomplicated because they were facing an attempt to overthrow and to cancel out the vast expansion of human rights of which the American Bill of Rights was the mother document. To kill the incontestable authority and autocratic rule from which their ancestors liberated them from more than two centuries ago in bravery with promise and sacrifice for them was a no-brainer.

The determination of Susan's generation to preserve liberty was as fixed and certain as the determination of that early generation of Americans to win it. Indeed, it was an effort that could go well only because those who have inherited the rewards of freedom did not lose the will to preserve their freedom first at home.

The Sun They Called the Moon`

When Franklin D. Roosevelt called out the four freedoms, it was as if a light was called down the mountain. The first bolt of lightning is freedom being of speech and expression everywhere in the world. The second being freedom of every person to worship God in his way everywhere in the world. The third being freedom from want which, translated into world terms, means economic freedom which will secure to every nation a healthy peacetime prosperity for its citizens everywhere in the world. The fourth was freedom from fear. The sound of freedom filled Susan and her generation with great joy and pride because it also was the fact it was their generation's fate, circumstance, or the hand of God that had chosen them as the instrument of the enabling truth of the indistinguishability of all human rights. For when fate itself must seek out in a disturbed world the quiet quality of mercy and its splendor in nobility, fate finds this nobility in the common person. Ordinary men and women, however ignorant, may walk with the knowledge of mercy; yet in the uppermost reaches, there is that which even the wise may not know. Nothing of the world is able to embrace truth, and were they to speak of it in its minuteness, nothing in the world is able to split the truth. The common men and women are histories chosen intermediaries to carry the embers of hope to places where hope has become feeble in spaces where hope has been destroyed in a world gone badly wrong in a world that sees the hand of darkness once again rise in it.

Susan and my father had not been sleeping well these last few nights. I would hear them get up in the middle of the evening and I would climb down and watch them in a dim kitchen light that shined in the overhead above the stove. In that same light objects appeared to lose their substance casting instead, shimmering shadows of pans dripping off the wall in strange configurations. At times, Susan and my father would talk, and other times I found them sitting; holding each other with Susan's head resting on his shoulder. The night's light poured over them like a hollow stream giving them dimension, revealing expressions of compassion that I heard in shallow sighs as I squatted with my knees in my arms on the stairs. I felt no suffering, the warmth of their faces gravitated to me and my frozen fears of the darkness thawed as I ran to them.

Chapter 4

Songs to Keep the Dark Away

Richard held on to the last key in the drawer. He pressed into it and the more he did, the more he began to remember what it opened. It was one of many keys belonging to the occupants of a house once shared with an assemblage of political activists. The key belonged to a spacious Victorian styled edifice of a house that had a prominent library room referred to by its residents as the meeting room. In that old study, he would sometimes starkly eye a poster that read, "Love is all you need," when meetings ran into long hours and moving a plan of things to be done and problems to be addressed felt more like being confined to moving around in a traffic circle.

The house was the local SDS house. These were not weekend hippies or armchair activists, but people so devoted they cut themselves off from family and friends for years. All its residents were members of Students for a Democratic Society, but not the old SDS. This new community was noted for meetings where people freely smoked and shared marijuana; where some but not all young men bore boisterous mustaches and some but not all young women seem to pay homage to a Western-cinéma vérité liveliness that finally became known as the New Left. They came marching through the canyons and hills of political activism in battalions and in multitudes of colors bursting in double-dip tie-dye tee shirts in denim blue jeans, jackets, and in brown leather buckskin boots.

These people were more often than not raised in the Midwest and Southwest, and their pastoral dress indicated a different tradition, one more adjusted to the frontier, more violent, more laissez-faire, more plain-knuckle boned, and more callus-handed, than that of the early SDS. They were non-Jewish, nonintellectual, and non-urbanized, from a secular class, and often without any family tradition of political activism, much less political theory. In fact, they tended to be not only ignorant of the history of The Left's urban center political positions, but also out-and-out uninterested in them.

In the year 1960, almost 50 percent of America's population was under 18 years of age. Thus setting the stage for a majority of young people to bring and bear new questions as to why in a country they held as free and open, why previously upheld structures of racism, sexism, and socioeconomic class were still all around them. Hence, race and alienation became the two principle axis points they used for their vision of a better America. At college campuses throughout the country, anger against these "Establishment's" structures incited both peaceful and violent protest.

The SDS held its first meeting in 1960 on the University of Michigan's campus in Ann Arbor, Michigan, where Alan Haber was elected president. Its political manifesto, known as the Port Huron Statement, was adopted at the organization's first convention in 1962 based on an earlier draft by staff member Tom Hayden.

The manifesto was a freshly forward-thinking ideology that was stark and progressive. The Port Huron Statement as it is called picked apart the political system of the United States for not achieving international peace and it picked apart Cold War foreign policy, the terror of nuclear war, and the arms race itself. In domestic matters, it damned racial discrimination, economic inequality, big businesses, trade unions, and political parties. In addition to its nitty-gritty criticism and analytic thinking of the American system, the manifesto also announced a chain of changes. It predicted a need to forge into two authentic political parties to achieve a stronger democracy, for firmer power for individuals through grassroots political organizations, more significant participation by workers in business management, and for an expanded public sector with enhanced public assistance, including a "program against poverty." The manifesto provided thoughts on what and how to bring social justice improvements, and encouraged nonviolent civil disobedience as the means by which students could bring forth a "participatory democracy."

In the university academic year 1962–1963, the President was Tom Hayden, the Vice President was Paul Booth, and the National Secretary was Jim Monsonis. There were nine chapters with, at most, about 1000 members. The national office in New York City existed on a few desks, some chairs in serious need of repair, a couple of file cabinets and a few typewriters. The SDS group with a strong belief in decentralization and distrust for most organizations did not have a strong central bureaucracy. Three advocates at the office, Don McKelvey, Steve Max, and the National Secretary, Jim Monsonis, operated the office through long hours with little pay to help the local chapters, and to help establish new ones. Most activities were orientating toward civil rights and the Student Nonviolent Coordinating Committee (SNCC) that played a key role in inspiring SDS.

By the end of the academic year at the annual convention at Pine Hill, New York, there were over 200 delegates from 32 different colleges and universities. There they decided to give more power to the chapters, who would then send delegates to the National Council. They would meet quarterly to handle the on-going business activity, and in the spirit of participatory democracy, a consensus was reached to elect new officers each year.

It was at this time that the Black Power Movement was first gaining some momentum before Stokely Carmichael made the movement more mainstream in 1966. But the change made it pathetic for white activists who expect to lead protests for black civil rights. This "into the ghetto" decision was a virtual failure, all the same, the fact that it existed at all pulled in many young idealists to SDS. Alternatively, SDS would attempt to organize white unemployed youths through a new program called the Economic Research and Action Project (ERAP).

Later in the fall of 1967, the New Left succeeded in increasing their anti-war actions. The draft had become an important issue on college campuses, and over the rest of the 1967 academic year, students started to attack university complicity in it, as the schools had begun to supply student's class rankings, used to determine who was to be drafted.

Then, on October 1, the University of California, Berkeley irrupted into the prominent and prolonged suffering that was the free speech movement. Led by a charismatic student activist, Mario Savio of Friends of SNCC, about three thousand students or more hemmed in a police car that attempted to take away a student, arrested for setting up a draft card-burning table in defiance of a ban by the University. The sit-down prevented the police car from moving for 32 hours. The demonstrations, meetings, and strikes that resulted all but shut the university down with hundreds of students arrested.

The campus at the University of Wisconsin in Madison on October 17 had its school year start with a massive demonstration against university complicity in the war in allowing the makers of Napalm, to recruit. Peaceful at first, the protest turned into a sit-in and was violently dispersed by the Madison police and riot squad, resulting in many injuries and arrests. A resulting mass student mobilization and a strike later closed the university for several days. A continuous organized chain of demonstrations against the draft led by members of the Resistance, the War Resisters League, and SDS added gas to the fire of opposition.

In Oakland, California on October 21, 1967, after conventional civil rights tactics of peaceful pickets failed, Stop the Draft Week ended in a massive hit and run skirmishes with the police. Organizers estimated 15,000 to 30,000 protesters were there, while the police gave informal estimates of 10,000 to 20,000. The huge 100,000 people, October 21 March on the Pentagon saw hundreds arrested and injured. Nighttime raids on draft offices began to spread.

By the late 1960s, the undeclared war in Vietnam had dragged on for four years despite promises from representative leaders that we had turned the corner. While these massive protest marches began to bring a moral sense to the issue by placing these matters at the forefront of the awareness and attention of millions of American people, they did little to stop the war.

Various in loco parentis manifestations began appearing on-campus that continued recruiting for the military and, again, taking part in the ranking for the draft.

Following the spring of 1968, National SDS activists led an effort on the campuses called

"Ten Days of Resistance," and local chapters cooperated with the Student Mobilization Committee in rallies, marches, sit-ins, and teach-ins reached a momentum on April 26 in a one-day strike. Approximately a million students boycotted classes that day making it the largest student strike in the history of the United States. Even so, the New York City-based national media mostly ignored it. Instead, it concentrated on a student shutdown on the Columbia University Campus in New York, led by an inter-racial alliance of Columbia SDS chapter activists and Student Afro Society activists. Because of the amount of media publicity given to Columbia SDS activists like SDS chairperson Mark Rudd during the Columbia Student Revolt, the SDS was on the map politically and became for a few years a household name in the United States.

Thus the organizational basis of the SDS, which had begun in the elite colleges, began to be extended to more institutions that were public. The theoretical foundation of the Revolutionary Youth Movement (RYM) was speeding outside of the college campus, understandings that most of the American population, including both students and the "middle-class," where being compromised, due to their relationship as legal instruments in a name only paper Constitution as their purpose and existence was to be a subordinate production working class. Once, no longer needed for that purpose, they might not have any equal rights with a class of property and privilege.

Students then could be workers gaining skills before employment, contrasting the old Progressive Labor thinking that considered students and employees as being in split constructs that could associate, but never jointly organize. On the contrary, SDS strongly felt that coordinating could extend to youth wholly including students, those serving in the military, and those unemployed.

If nothing else, SDS also exposed the FBI's sinister Cointelpro program, an attempt to infiltrate and destroy left-wing organizations. Cointelpro program (an acronym for Counter Intelligence Program) was a series of covert and often illegal projects conducted by the United States Federal Bureau of Investigation (FBI) aimed at surveillance, infiltrating, discrediting, and disrupting domestic political organizations.

Cointelpro tactics included discrediting targets by psychological warfare, planting false reports in the media, smearing by forged letters, harassment, wrongful imprisonment, extralegal violence and assassination and political repression.

In August of 1969 Fred Hampton, national representative for the Black Panther Party, was assassinated by members of the Chicago Police Department, as part of a Cointelpro operation. "We expected about twenty Panthers to be in the apartment when the police raided the space. Only two of those black nigger fuckers were killed," Fred Hampton and Mark Clark." —FBI Special Agent Gregg York.

During the 1968-69 academic year membership in SDS chapters around the United States increased dramatically.

"We felt that doing nothing in a period of repressive violence is itself a form of violence. That is the part that I think is the hardest to understand. If you sit in your house, live your white life and go to your white job, and allow the country that you live in, to murder people and to commit genocide, and you sit there, and

you don't do anything about it, that's violence."
—Naomi Esther Jaffe (born 1943) is a former undergraduate student of Herbert Marcuse and former member of the Weather Underground Organization. Jaffe was recently the Executive Director of Holding Our Own, a multiracial foundation for women.

The "Days of Rage," two months after the assassination of Fred Hampton in August of 1969 the Weather Underground Organization, (WUO) conducted their first public demonstration on October 8, 1969, in Chicago timed to coincide with the trial of the Chicago 7.

The Weathermen and subsequently the Weather Underground Organization was a radicalized American left organization. In 1969, it splintered as a faction out of Students for a Democratic Society (SDS) made up of the national office leadership of SDS and their supporters. Their objective was to create a clandestine revolutionary party.

By the early 70s, Richard Nixon was President, the war had escalated to Laos and Cambodia, students were murdered protesting at Kent State, over 30,000 Americans, and countless more Vietnamese were dead with no end of the war in sight. Frustration with non-violent attempts to stop the killing, impatient with years of non-violence action plans with no result while being radicalized by the continuous escalating casualty count and the hearing disorder exhibited by publicly elected leaders that drove them to "bring the war home" more radicalized militant groups, as well as The Weathermen and Black Panthers, began to emerge.

The Weathermen theorize, "oppressed peoples" are the creators of the riches of empire, and it is to them that it belongs." "The goal of revolutionary struggle must be the control and use of this wealth in the interest of the oppressed peoples of the world."

With revolutionary positions characterized by Black separatist rhetoric, the group conducted a campaign of bombings through the mid-1970s. The bombing attacks mostly targeted government buildings and banks. After the explosion of a homemade bomb in Greenwich Village, NY in 1970 had killed three of their members, they determined that no one should die because of their direct action and no one did. Their actions were preceded by evacuation warnings, along with communiqués identifying the particular issue that the attack was intended to protest. For the bombing of the United States Capitol on March 1, 1971, they issued a communiqué saying it was in protest of the US invasion of Laos.

Richard had a unique ideological and personal relationship with many of the Weathermen through the Venceremos Brigade, a program he took part in as a student at the University of Washington in Seattle that involved US students volunteering to work in the sugar harvest in Cuba. The program was a common factor in the background of both Richard and the founders of the Weather Underground, with China a secondary influence.

The world surrounding them in the late 1960s endured a growing political activism movement through political protest in the United States and a worldwide struggle that had anti-manifest destiny energies on the march in Vietnam, Algeria, and Angola. Richard shared the belief they were on the winning side of history — creating new communities free from capitalist exploitation and embracing the Che Guevara prediction that many Vietnam-type conflicts would bring down the ascendancy of support in the United States for fascistic monopolistic developing regimes in the world and topple an immorally bankrupt war machine that was sending them. They believed that these types of urban guerrilla actions would act as a catalyst for a revolution. Many international events seemed to affirm the Weathermen's overall contention that worldwide revolution was imminent.

It was the time of the turbulent Cultural Revolution in China. It was the time of the 1968 student revolts in France, Mexico City, and elsewhere; the Prague Spring; the Northern Ireland Civil Rights Association; the emergence of the Tupamaros organization in Uruguay; the emergence of the Guinea-Bissauan Revolution within the United States. It was the time of the prominence of the Black Panther Party together with a series of "ghetto rebellions" throughout poor black neighborhoods across the country.

The Weathermen tried to recruit new members to set into motion a nationwide revolt against the government of that time. The members of the Weathermen targeted high school as well as college students, presuming they would be willing to rebel against the authoritative figures, including cops, principals, and bosses. They wanted to develop roots within the class struggle, targeting white working-class youths. The draft age members of the working class became the centering of the organizing effort because the working-class youths acutely felt the repressiveness effects of the military draft, low-wage jobs, and schooling. Schools became a common place of recruitment for the movement.

In direct actions, dubbed, "Jailbreaks" was the belief that school was where the young were reduced by the system because they were being conditioned to tolerate society's faults instead of questioning and rebelling against them. By them confronting state and corporate power, the odds were that they would see a freer society that would not land them on the FBI's ten most wanted list. In the manifesto compiled by Bill Ayers, Bernardine Dohrn, Jeff Jones, and Celia Sojourn, entitled "Prairie Fire," young people are channeled, coerced, misled, miseducated, and misused in the school setting. It is in schools that the youth of the nation become alienated from the authentic processes of learning about the world.

Members directed action against established leaders in government to expose a pattern of injustice that existed in the United States and abroad due to America's cynical and counter poisoning domestic and foreign policies. They also encouraged people to resist reliance upon their given privilege and to rise and take arms if necessary.

Consequently, if people tolerated the unjust actions of the state, they became complicit in those actions. According to "Prairie Fire," Weathermen explained that their intention was to encourage the people and provoke leaps in confidence and consciousness in an attempt to stir the imagination, organize the masses, and join in the people's day-to-day struggles in every way possible.

The Seattle Freedom Front, or SFF, was a radical anti-Vietnam War movement, based in Seattle, Washington, in the United States. The group, founded by then-University of Washington visiting philosophy professor and political activist Michael Lerner, carried out its protest activities from 1970 to 1971. The most famous members of the SFF were the "Seattle Eight" — Eight SFF members charged with "conspiracy to incite a riot" in the wake of a violent protest at a courthouse.

A couple of months later, on April 16, a federal grand jury indicted eight members of the SFF on charges of setting off the February 17 riot. The FBI in an infiltration of the Weather Underground later arrested one of the eight, Richard, in San Francisco, California. Federal District Judge George Bolt was assigned the case, which began in his Tacoma courtroom on November 6, 1970. The trial quickly ran off track by the defendants' vocal disruptions, a protest walkout, and their eventual refusal to sit down.

Bolt declared a mistrial on December 10, 1970. Citing all defendants for contempt of court, Judge Bolt immediately found the eight guilty of contempt, sentenced them to six months in prison, and denied to grant bail. The defendants finally served three months in prison.

The original charges of inciting a riot and conspiracy to damage the Seattle Courthouse are unsuccessfully prosecuted. Most who witnessed the trial agreed that the prosecution's case was struggling with the admission of government witnesses on the stand that swore under oath they would go to any length to fight the activists. It is believed that the Seattle 8 would have been freed had they not infuriated the elderly judge with catcalls during the proceedings.

The day after, roughly 2,000 protesters assembled to escalate their dissent into violence, throwing rocks and paint at the courthouse and at police responding to the scene. Twenty are hurt in the riot, and 76 are arrested. In March 1970, the Seattle Front, UW Black Student Union, and the Weathermen organized hundreds of protesters at the University of Washington's campus. The group's demands are for the university to cut its athletic affiliations with Brigham Young University, a Mormon school that was accused of racism. Seattle Freedom Front and Black Student Union protagonists initiated a riot that went through eleven buildings at the University of Washington's Seattle campus. Approximately 200 chanting demonstrators left a trail of damage across the campus.

Chapter 5

The Brumal Moon

Each house was distinctive but attractive enough to make a pleasant-looking neighborhood. The population was about 500. In this inner circle, there was little crime. You never went on trips alone without someone making sure you returned safely. Educated enough about drugs like marijuana and impertinent enough to say, what else could they lie about? Realizing lies, seeing truth untouched by society's locking pliers came to them as natural as a person who farms land predicting the rain out of the dark and cloudy sky.

Despite living in a nation where misleading and well-educated men exploit fear, most could not forget what they instinctively knew. When history has to repeat the same warning, the rebukes that go with the warning grow boulder like a bell in a tower growing louder.

The Sun They Called the Moon`

The signal each time sent becomes stronger for those who seek to achieve the power set aside for a free people. But follow no law of God, nature, or country, only instead dedicate themselves to fear and not the death of it, placing them on the ancient path that they tread with their own feet leading them time, but time again to their own grave.

The doors of neighborhood houses forming a community within the town were left unbolted, windows left unlocked as if indicating a new beginning as if the wall that kept neighbor from neighbor could finally yield to the end of fear, the dust of time, and eventually crumble. It existed in what seems to have been for only a moment, fleeting and fading like sunlight on the grass, but in that tome of a morning Nimbus caught between sleep and awakening they heard an ascendant like a voice that called to them to remember, and they answered suddenly, I know you.

The breeze blew through his hair. Richard is silent. His stare is silent. The eyes in his head flow slowly across the western geography as if following some slow, thirsty river knocked out of place by the finger of God as the river runs after it. He deliberately stares as if he is following currents of people from a city high-rise, watching them below as they flow across congested streets escaping into a land beyond its border's frame and out to some forgiving sea. His mind pushes out and then pulls in memories.

"Revolution! Revolt before we die, brother, Revolution!"

"He's been out there for almost an hour," said Beth in a nerve-racking voice looking to find a louder record to put on.

"He's a basket case," said Macy, leaning on the window's ledge with one hand and the other holding the drapery aside. "Look at him, the man he's out there. Wow, is there life on Mars spaceman?"

"Don't," said Betty passing a lit joint to Beth. "He's freaked; the meathead doesn't know his limitations. The crazies are nothing to joke about."

"I can't disagree with the politics," replied Macy, still watching him. "Poor bastard, look, look! He's started a fire on the road."

"Revolution, Revolt brother before it's too late! You call yourselves revolutionaries!"

"What a strange voice this; the guy has," said Macy. "He's got an audience; everyone is on their lawns. Pam, John, there's Peter."

"Who is he? Anyone we know?" asked Beth, walking over to Richard walking through the screen door.

"No," answered Richard, standing on the front porch.

"There goes Hiker and Pete from across the road," said Macy. He ran over to join them. "The way this guy keeps sounding off he might be looking to get the attention of The House on Un-

American Activities Committee. This is going to be something I don't want to miss, hey," He continued, engaging Betty moving across the lawn.

The flames blazed upward, making everyone uneasy and tense. The sight of erupting, disorientating, and freakish images cast out everywhere reached inward to the cold internal temperature of the early representation of fear of shadows. The shadow, he cast engulfed the street and walls of the houses, flickering madly as a boy who seemed to summon the fire from the pitch-blackness. The trees cast shimmering shades taking on a life to all their dancing in a primitive auburn glare, trapped as if in some primitive preordination with reality itself.

"The flames," said Betty as she stood mesmerized with a look that was as distant as the usual tone of her voice.

"There she goes," said Beth. "Don't get all spooky."

"That's right, somebody go get the marshmallows, instead," said Macy.

"He soaks up an influence from the flames," said Betty, "It rages as he rages. It breathes with his breath."

"Got to hand it to you, Betty," said Macy.

"I won't be scared of you. Stop it, you witch! Are you trying to scare me?" asked Beth. Betty returned a smirk.

"No, no, look, he's on fire, see," said Macy. "It's alright he's jumping around. He got a hot foot. I bet he is chewing over his decisions right about now."

"Isn't someone going to try to help him out?" asked Snow White. No sooner than the words flew out of her mouth, people began, picking up handfuls of dirt to put him out.

"It's amazing, now, he's reasonable, now. It is amazing how sensible you get once you've been on fire," Macy said to Richard, helping him with the garden hose. Later, the two men walked back together. Beth and Betty left to meet them on the front porch with the others, John, and Pam as the fire lay smoldering without fuel, and a man lay next to it wasted.

They all entered the house and went into the big room they called, the meeting room. Beth went to turn on the stereo. Pam, Sara, and Sam turned on the lamp and lit candles of different shapes. The candles were of a variety you could find today in a specialty shop in the more trending small New England towns at least the ones that appealed to the occasional excursionists looking for some historical sustenance from America's first revolution down by the Freedom Trail. The candles were handmade by Beth and Snow White who later carved out a business in Vermont selling their candles to former New York City dwellers that took to the woods; each color of the candles had its meaning. Royal blue: promoting laughter and joviality; loyalty, light blue: the spiritual color, helpful in devotional or inspirational meditations bringing peace and tranquility and radiating Aquarius energy. Blue: Primary spiritual color; for obtaining wisdom, harmony, inner light, peace; truth and guidance.

"Let's do a joint," said Beth, pacing nervously." I need something to calm me down."

"A joint, that's a good idea, go ahead," said Macy, "Do you feel all right?" he asked, looking at Snow White, turning almost as white as her frost colored hair.

"I'm ok," said Snow White. She kicked off her sandals.

"Turn off the stereo," said Richard, standing by the screen door. Hiker turned down the stereo and took a joint from Betty.

"What the hell, what just happened?" asked John. They all began to gather. Some on super-sized comfortable pigmented beanbags and others simply sat and crossed their legs on the floor waiting for Richard to give his thinking on what happened. Richard had stepped back out to see if the guy whose pant leg caught on fire was going to be all right.

"He looks like he's going to be okay," said Richard, over the sound of the screen door's spring as he opened the door.

"Somebody, tell me what the fuck happened," Betty shouted, tossing her arms up and vexing, ricocheting up from her sitting position.

"I'll tell you what happened," replied Macy. "He's another Harold. Another one who is going to get us all killed." Everyone laughed at the mention of Harold's name. "You remember Harold, the guy who wanted to join us and the "Revolution." When some of you wondered, why I said to turn him down, I said he's dangerous or some FBI plant which would be the same thing."

"He was not dangerous or and FBI guy," said Hiker.

"No, he wasn't an FBI guy," said John.

"But he was dangerous," said Richard.

"Skinny Harold, You're kidding?" questioned Beth.

"That guy couldn't find his way around with a map," added Pete with a laugh.

"But he was dangerous," repeated Richard. "He was dangerous to himself, and that made him dangerous to everyone. He took it on himself when we rejected him. He decided to become a one-man revolution."

"What's so dangerous? Come on, what kind of chump-head decides to rob a bank and leaves the bag," said Macy, followed by most of them bursting out in laughter.

"That's not it, he rode there on his two-wheeler," added Pam, extending the joke to more laughter.

"Harold and his banana bar bike," said John, chuckling, "I couldn't believe it when they told me."

"They caught him on a hill," added Macy, howling with laughter. "His legs gave out."

"What about the bag, the bag." said Beth "He not only left the bag of money. He left his name. It was sewn in the bag."

"When he got off the bike and started to run the cop called him by his name, 'Harold stop.' When he hears him shout, 'Harold is that you?' the guy stops running and is completely confused that the cop knows him well enough to call him by name," said John.

"Seven, seven years," called out Snow White.

"A guy who never did anything to anyone got seven years in a federal hell hole for trying to help us because he believed we are right and our government is wrong," said Richard. "Wrong in how they wage war without the consent of those who have to pay," he continued. "Wrong in the running over the enabling rights of a democratic and free people whose only crime is to ask their government, what the hell are you doing?

Wrong in actively making sure that the answer to the question is never heard by way of intimidation and assassination of its people. Harold believes this is wrong and this is what we believe is wrong. So what are we laughing at? Are we laughing at who we are or laughing at who we are not? I can't keep it straight anymore, but we are not animals," said Richard, and the atmosphere of jocularity ended.

Harold could have easily been mistaken for a boy or a girl but never a man. He had black hair running down to the small of his back, frizzy like mohair wool. It fanned out across his back like an umbrella left unclasped at the bottom. You could have easily mistaken him on his bike wearing his black badly battered white spotted hockey helmet for a modest -looking tall young tomboy of a girl riding carefree down the road not yet acutely aware that nature was being a little late and like a father; you did not feel sorry for him. Only some inward tug needing to protect the years, the weeks, or days before nature made the change, forever.

He had the awkward look of adolescents. Nature for some reason left the boy in him. In an around campus, the story was that he had skipped a few grades in high school and was an ultra-smart kid, but he was not. Because of his late maturation, it was hard for him to develop close friends. He compensated by trying to join every organization on campus that would take him. He was a good kid late to nature's party. It was the good in him that made him want to join the SSD house.

John and Betty immediately notice the temperature drop in the group's common bond. They both eyed Richard with a sudden disdain.

"Our job now is to lead white kids into armed revolution? We never intended for Harold to spend the next five to seven years in jail," said John, bristling at the suggestion that they should have let Harold in the program when Richard agreed to keep him out.

"Ever since SDS became revolutionary," said Betty, "we've been able to prove how it's achievable to defeat the frustration and impotence by fighting to reclaim the government by any means necessary for the people. Kids across this country know where the lines are drawn. The revolution is touching all of our lives now."

Moreover, said Pete, by this government's contemptuousness for the will of the people tens of thousands have learned that protest and marches don't cut it anymore. We must introduce their violence to our own to defend our sacred and undeniable human rights and create a blow to this stolen government so great in strength that a government of the people spills out of it again, backed by the will of the citizens. Violence is the only thing that registers in the thick heads of these ignorant thugs who beat on the heads of their people with such reckless abandon and with no legal authority under our written Constitution."

"How far do you think you can take this violent thing, what do you think peace is going to look like at this price to the rest of the world when they start to put us all in a grave?" asked Richard. "Man, how can peace come out of violence to revenge unreasonable conduct, but through the grave? So before, you run down the road where violence meets vengeance don't forget what the Dzogchen masters said about the path of violence. What you do not like when done to yourself, do not do to others. Best then to dig two graves once you get there, one for your enemy and one for yourself."

"Unlike Richard," said Hiker, I don't question our tactics, not after many petitions and the demonstrations we all sat in. Moreover, what was their response to our peaceful assembly? We wind up defenseless giving up our bodies to the sadistic fascists, whaling their batons on our heads, bleeding out on a sidewalk street like batted animals for sport; I was willing to go to prison, I did. To me, there is no question of what has to happen to stop the greater violence that is going on."

"First, we carried out symbolic acts of extreme vandalism directed at monuments to war, racism, and then we attacked property," said Betty, "but never will we set upon the people in violence like a bunch of angry dogs! We were born to respect human life. We show our outrage, and demonstrate our determination to topple by any means necessary the illegitimate occupying government and to end all economic violence through physical violence when necessary."

"They're the ones who changed the rules, man, from civil discourse to violence, not us. We didn't tear apart the United States Constitution and the Bill of Rights by waging an illegal war and suppressing the will and the rights of the people. We are not the ones who force the people to live in a lie. I didn't think I had to point it out to you Richard that they're lying through their teeth to our faces," said Pam.

The Sun They Called the Moon`

"When the people tolerate the unjust actions of the State, they become complaisant in creating an unfair State," said Snow White.

"Don't you get it, it's over," said Richard, "They didn't only take away our rights in a cynical attempt to control the country. They are changing us too. We started this thing to make a better way so we must be the better men and women, if not we are going to get people killed. We own the responsibility for the dangers we presented to others in some of our final choices. The choices that result in these weighted unintended consequences never leave can never leave our thoughts for long, and now you want to escalate. They are the escalators of war and demented violence, not us. How can we become our worst enemy?

Our honesty once apparent is fading fast and so is the way by which we once directed ourselves. Our openness is the means to the self-completion of our purpose because sincerity affects others in a way it can change them. The movement with all its sincerity, all its sacrifice, and resoluteness in ending the violence without an action to violence produced changes; and without any effort, it will accomplish its purpose without being drawn into meeting force with violence."

"Richard, we understand what you're saying," said Peter. He began to stand up having the attention of everyone on the floor. He continued, "The movement is transitioning to an important an unmistakable task toward making this a real revolution. The work we are doing with others across the country is in response to a government lying to and shooting down its people. Consequently, we engage in with good cause the creation of a mass revolutionary movement. At this point in our history, an underground revolutionary party is out of the question. A revolutionary mass movement is different from the conventional politics of a mass based activist sympathizer protest movement. When the government starts to shoot down middle- class peaceful protestors, it dramatically ends the peaceful protest movement. Richard is correct, but it's not going to end in the way this current government thinks it will because of who we have been, who we are, and who we will always be, a free people.

Moreover, it is kindred to our first revolution, and it is inborn. Take the Red Guard in China, based on the full participation and involvement of masses of people applying and making revolution; not a peace movement, that's gone, but a revolution with a full willingness to participate in the violent, but necessary struggle to throw out an immoral and illegal government."

"We're going to shove the war down their throats," added Macy. "And I promise you someday we will show while we're at it, how much better we are as a free people, both tactically and morally in an all-out revolution against an illegal government. The fascist U.S. corporate ideology, we are going to bring the war home, and we are going to kick their ass."

The next morning Snow White woke up early, walked in, and sat with her legs folded in a chair. The morning sun through an open window broke off her naked shoulder casting her shadow to the floor; "You're not going to leave without saying goodbye are you?" she asked. "It's too soon."

The Sun They Called the Moon`

"Like every good goodbye it's better to be gracious and leave before being asked to leave," said Richard. His words have respect to his actions, and his actions have respect to his words as he picked up her chin. Stooping down for his two backpacks, and then opening the screen door Richard passed through it as the one note sound of the spring's extending recoil faded to the sounds of a common day. He does not desire to go beyond this. Snow White ran after him, standing next to him as Richard put one backpack in the seat. The other he tied to a rack on the hood. Suddenly embracing him, she held him tight to her chest for so long; it was ending. She held him for the last time, and it seemed to them their closest moment in that their time was all too early. In those moments, they both realizing it had to end all of it ending all too soon.

The sun, shone on the small driveway as it lit the clear sky as it does after a storm turning the sky a dark shade of blue. The cumulus clouds as white as snow were in motion, appearing as upheld faraway lands lost within the blue of the horizon as the car drove away from the sun. Silence filled the small car, the kind that chokes on hellos and goodbyes. He looked out the window as if searching for the perfume of ice on a hot and dusty day.

Telephone poles move quickly. Everything moved too fast. Hills rolled by, the sun burnt hot and rose as warm air blew dry his face, riding north to the city asking himself questions he was not sure of pass housing tenements, the shopping center, and ramps; not turning to look back, no time to go back. Is it worth leaving everything behind? What did I leave behind he asked himself, passed the storage tanks, junkyards, and trailer parks? He looked out over the vast indistinguishability of the freeway and felt cast down into a disturbance of ineptitude, pass the furnaces and the industrial parks.

Richard put the key into a small plastic bag, closed the drawer, and left his house for the last time and headed for the airport.

Chapter 6

A World in the Throes of the Frozen Moon

I awoke to a soft caress on my forehead and the tone of my mother's voice.

"Billy, wake up," said Susan as I wiped the sleep from my eyes. "We overslept for school."

I was in no hurry to get dressed. "Did dad go to work yet?" I asked.

"Yes," answered Susan. She walked out the door.

I started to dress as the morning sun rose upon the new-made snow left during the night. I looked out my window on the second floor then flung open the window, heard the dumb weights drop like a sledgehammer in the walls on to something, never figured out what, nevertheless, wishing it would drop on the hissing radiator that kept me erratically awake all night. I stuck my head out the window to escape the heat, and at that moment, I came up with an entirely new theory of why so many people hate hissing snakes.

When I took my breath of crisp cool air, it was like drinking cold, clean water from an untouched stream. Then I began to notice how the snow silhouetted every single misshapen tree bark and bent branch, dressing crouched branches in a snow powder that stuck to them like a gossamer glove.

The trees surrounded the old New England Colonial house like watchtower sentries on a look out, caught off their guard at the break of dawn, their branches, stiletto-like and intimidating. Like defeated and disfigured necromancers with swords, beguiling the sunlight to bend into razor sharp coated water ice to stab the north wind and then it did until it moaned and bellowed.

The Sun They Called the Moon`

It was as if nature having a particular temper and disposition became startled and frenzied at the sight of branches as if hands, elongated to arms, atrophied by rivers of light and by the white star fires flaring off their glistening fingernails, awakened the winds of Thor by the bright light entranced in water ice of reflected starlight. Vast magnificent twisted sheets of snow flashed-frozen before me in endless waves across a majestic white sea trapped in unsparing silence but for the sound of the one-note song from the lighthouse harboring me in its solitary long-distance call to the arms of the ocean through the din of the weathering sea.

As I dressed all I could suppose is that, no one moves their kid to a new school in January, a private, parochial school.

A Parochial school's fundamental nature is very distinctive from their public school counterpart. The Parochial school is in effect a school concentrating on developing of individuals in a central ethical code that says we are one body and hence on an individual basis created the same on a shared planet.

The Sun They Called the Moon`

This thought likewise has the distinct nature in the parochial school of seeming unworldly drawing its authority from meditation on the natural or unnatural state of man. It is based on a system of principles governing morality, and then acceptable conduct is reinforced through western Christian Jew Dao faith, empowering both faith and education to where individuals are to develop themselves: intellectually, physically, socially, emotionally, and of course, spiritually. These core beliefs are an essential element of the course of study, and the condition is implicit in any action for social justice.

Catholic schools are the largest non-public school system in the United States. The thinking is the schools have been critical in the development of the American culture in particular at the end of World War II in the Post-war development era and the Cold War when enrollment of Americans in these parochial schools was at its highest.

"Will you let go!" I said, pulling my arm away from my little sister, Katie. My sister didn't know what to make of all this moving around we did recently. She was prepared as well as she could be for her new school but, not for anything like this. She was holding tightly to the cuffs of my coat as we walked through the snow to find the right telephone pole that was the bus stop to wait for school bus seventy-seven.

"Hey, will you let go," I said, again, pulling my arm away from my little sister's hold, but no sooner than it's down, it's up again. "Will you let go, cut it out, will ya!" The snow that clung to the trees was falling, but not my sisters' hand and arm clinging to me. Katie's tight grasping was like trying to detach a magnet from a piece of metal. We both walked down the snow covered deserted street that had its one street lamp go off as we passed under it.

"Katie, cut it out. Let go of my sleeve," I said, loud enough to hear the echo of my voice being smothered up in the eerily silence made by the sleepy snow covered homes that seemed to soak up all sound as we passed. The muffled sound of the silence and the funny sounding distant foghorn startled me. I suddenly no longer minded her grasp. We walked to the right telephone pole and waited there for our bus.

The seaside road was long and winding. I watched a pair of head lights grow larger in the twilight of the dawn's mist for the longest time until it rattled up to us like some junk heap about to explode. We both leaped back as if it would, but it rolled passed us. We were like two lone specks on miles of road stretching over an open field of a snow meadow hill, not a damn thing moving except for my knees trembling involuntarily from the cold winds penetrating my pants like an icy dry leaf scratching crosswise passing sluggishly across the top of the snow's frozen white tundra.

As if the cold wasn't bad enough, I felt like I had eaten too much "Butterflied Shrimp". I thought of running, but my parents might have as well moved us to the island of Alcatraz. Those nuns, I thought to myself, they had to send me to a nun school. I'm going to a school full of holy people. I'll be on my knees, kneeling in front of statues. The school must smell like the inside of a church, I thought.

The Sun They Called the Moon`

There was something or someone that appeared down the distant road like a blue speck walking relentlessly towards us. As the speck got closer, it slowly revealed itself as a boy. Soon I could hear a faint whistling, then a tune. A carefree bounce began to appear in his stride, and I noticed he was wearing the same blue sports jacket I was wearing. He had a round pudgy face and brown hair. He finally landed on the square foot of snowy ground next to me. My sister who still had her hand fused to me tried to hide from this morning Whistler by shyly standing behind me and only peeking out at times with her dark eyes from the side of my ribcage as he whistled his tune. He was almost half my size. He stood next to me and waited, still whistling freely as if by himself.

Great, I thought. The only human around this early in the morning and it had to be a whistler, a short, pudgy whistler. It was awkward, no one around for miles and we're pretending not to notice each other in front of this stupid telephone pole that has its light still lit. This went on until a car had spun to and away from us, about three minutes.

"Hey, we got the same uniform. You must be going to my school," he said, a little late but I wished I had said something sooner.

"I hope you're not going to be in my room. Naw, I was just kidding," he said. Great, I thought, just what I need a comedian. "Who's the little monkey holding your arm?"

I looked down to my sister's face, and she looked up at me with two pools of dark eyes and a blue French cap that was about to fall off. She's my sister, Katie. Leave her alone," I said, abruptly.

"Ok, ok man, you don't have to get all uppity about it," he replied, showing the palms of his hands.

"Just don't mess with her, ok," I said. Katie got a little brave and loosened her hand as if she were thinking about clocking him herself.

"Aw right already. He's got a sister complex," he said. A short silence came to us as we waited for a car in the distance to reach and passed us. "What's your name?"

"Will, what's yours?" I asked.

"My name, my name is Greg Tarantino," said Greg Tarantino. The bus pulled up in front of us, and it was empty. We were the first stop. Well, see ya later. You really are in for it now." said Greg.

I stepped on the bus and sat in the middle of the bus with Katie. Greg Tarantino sat in the last seat of the empty school bus. As I rode on the bus, I felt the pounding of my heart and the sweat in my palms with each new face that got on. They all knew each other from the years before and seemed to be friendly. As if didn't have enough to handle, what can this kid mean? I was in for it. How could I get in trouble so fast? I thought it might be my tie. I quickly undid it and retied it from memory as best I could for someone who only that morning got his first lesson in tying a necktie. I sat with what I thought was an enormous knot at my throat.

The bus pulled into the campus and drove the long way around by way of an extended circular route on the campus grounds rolling past snow covered athletic fields. I sat quietly looking out the window as the campus spread out all around me. The Academy exteriors are built out of the same burnt colored bricks of dark brown, red, and orange as if peering back at me through the bus window like leaves of an autumn tree in the sun. I saw the elementary, the junior high school, and the high school buildings clearly differentiated by their unclouded gold leaf emblazed names as the bus slowly rolled by them. That's how I knew when to walk Katie off the bus. I got off the bus's last step with Katie still holding on like a vise, and now she seemed more frighten than ever. I went up to a nun and told her where my sister was going and she detached us and took her by the hand around the corner of her new school. Katie turned to me with an expression of abandonment. I stepped back on the bus.

The Sun They Called the Moon`

We finally pulled into a stop in front of the school I was attending. It seemed strange to see so many people dressed the same in one place. The school was T-shaped. The front of the school extended its stem in detail length to the back where you could see three sets of classrooms on each floor. On the left side of the front of the school building was the name of the patron saint and next to it a large cross. I could see the back of an old church resting at a distance in front of the campus facing the public street.

The schoolyard brimmed with cheerful voices. All the students entering the yard dressed the same, laughing loudly as if a Pied Piper called a tune and as he played, they jumped and danced. There was a sunken lot that had enough room for five baseball fields and a hidden stream that ran parallel to both the church and the school. The bell rang, I felt like I had swallowed a bowling ball. I was just standing there as they moved with the nimbleness of an excited school of fish and they were gone. I soon found myself alone.

Chapter 7

Sisters on the Watchtowers

Suddenly I faced two sisters. In the Catholic Church, a nun is a woman who has taken solemn vows (the male equivalent is a "monk" or "friar. In the various branches of the Benedictine tradition, sisters take vows to remain a member of a single monastic community in a conversion of modus vivendi to poverty and chastity.

Most monastic orders of sisters follow the two vows, with some orders taking an additional vow related to a specific work like teaching or character of their order. When a woman enters a convent, monastery, or abbey, she begins an initial period of testing the monastic life for six months to a year. This is the called the postulancy. If she, and the order she is in determines that she has a calling to a monastic life, she receives the habit of that order, but the habit is a modification.

The headpiece worn pinned over the coif head coverings is a white veil instead of a black, to distinguish her from professed nuns and could be worn down to cover the face or up to expose it. Second, she undertakes the novitiate. The novitiate is a time span to last for two years living the life of a nun without taking vows. When she completes this period she may take her initial, temporary vows. Temporary vows last one to three years and are evaluated for not less than three years, but not more than six. Ultimately, she will petition to make her "perpetual profession," taking permanent, solemn vows.

The two nuns I faced were dissimilar in dress. One sported a white veil, a lovely face, and an infectious smile. The other nun stood staunchly at about five feet and wore a black veil with a reddened face all but irrupting in indignation. "What do you think you're doing, Buster?" she asked.

"Ahh, I, I," I replied, trying to find my brain.

"I thought so," she said with a look on her face that had an exuberant satisfaction on it like a baseball pitcher nodding to the catcher after putting one over the plate. I stood there in a daze.

"Sister, I haven't seen this one before," said the nun with the white veil as she leans down into my face and smiled.

"Sure, that's, that's, the one who was late last week and I had to send him to the office, but this time buster, I'm going to send you to the moon," the heavyset nun with the black veil said staring into my eyes like a scrutinizing chef inspecting a head of lettuce for a chicken salad. "What are you doing out here after the first bell?" The two bushes she had for eyebrows, jumped.

"I am a little lost," I replied, explaining the existential dilemma in relation to my current anxiety and values in personal identity as best I could at my age.

"Wait a minute, he's a new one," said the nun with the white veil. "What's your name?"

"Will," I said.

"Will, I am Sister Carolyn, and this is Sister Christine just follow us," she said, cheerily.

Nevertheless, Sister Christine looked skeptically back over her shoulders as if still trying to recognize me as the person she sent to the office for being late last week. Looking for any sign that I was making the whole thing up, double-checking to see if I was still there. I had the feeling she was expecting me to make a run for it. All the same, running would be futile I thought. The sneakers she wore were not for her health.

"I heard that we were getting a transfer," Sister Carolyn said, facing front and speaking as if I were walking in front of her. "You are looking for room 57-A, down the hall."

The corridor was a sickly green color and had a smell of fresh vomit and ammonia evaporating into the air adding to my stomach-turning feeling. The building had only two temperatures. One was tropical heat, the other bone-chilling cold, and it did not help that today the building was at the tropical heat temperature.

I began to feel the bowling ball in my stomach turn into a swamp monster. I knew of no bigger misadventure. I wished I was anywhere but where I was. I came to the door of room 57-A pale as a powder. I knocked, what jarhead knocks before going into a classroom?

"Come in," I heard the teacher say. It was a bolt from the blue to see a real live adult person that morning and at such a close distance. My mind went away on vacation and left me watching him at the desk. I peeked to the left, and my gawk of a facial expression met fifteen to twenty-five faces staring back with equal astonishment. "Let see," he said going through his attendance sheets. "Ah, you must be Will." The sweat pouring off my forehead and face made that obvious. I was malfunctioning like a dishwasher. Giggles came up like a slow ripple from the class and then hit me as if I was standing on a sidewalk, and a burst of cold water from a road puddle splashed me. I tripped, thus continuing my morning imitation of a rainbow by turning into the color of embarrassment. "Will, he said, "take the last desk in this row," pointing to it with a nod of his head and gesturing with the class's attendance book. The desk in the back seemed remote. I walked passed everyone in what seemed an endless ride through an awkward circumstance. The wool jacket I was wearing didn't help me as I perspired extravagantly. The class of twenty-five odd faces turned to follow me to my seat with their fifty odd eyes. I walked to the back of the entire class passing whispers of look how tall. My lanky legs felt rubberized. I was changing color more times than a retina displays on a new smartphone.

"That's the kid I was telling you about," said Greg with a gleeful smile," The one at my bus stop."

I wasn't this tall in my other school. There was even a girl taller than I was and a couple of guys. So what's the big crime about being tall, get a life, people. I wanted to hide, under the desk and I would have if I thought I could fit.

"Hey, Will, before today I was the brand-new guy. Welcome and welcome to new person status. We try not to sweat over small stuff in here. We distinguish every person as a cool person and no better than anyone else. We tend to be a little informal in this classroom. We all go by first names in here. By the way, Will, you can call me Richard," said Richard.

Chapter 8

To the Ends of the Moon

When a journey is a reward, there is also the heart's passage to love. The progress to the reward of where and whose heart must also be must lie in a reward of the journeying toward love for what is true never changes. It is as constant as the stars in the summer's sky to those who see it. Sometimes it is indescribable, and there are times it is unexplainable. All journeys are ultimately trips to self-awareness and the reawakening of the knowledge of where we are and what we are forever. It is an odyssey without time, space, distance, or matter. This is because truth is a condition that cannot be recognized but only shared through love.

The class stared at Richard as if he was a person of celebrity, a rock star. Richard had hair reaching down about four inches from the nape of his neck giving it a perception of length. He parted it in a flat grooved pompadour mullet from the center to the back of his head, twisting the hair upward tightly in tidy French rolls and low like a ponytail, but far more mature than a ponytail and far classier than a revolutionary era pigtail, tightening the side of the rolls. Richard eased back in leather boots and jeans, placing two hands flat behind him on the front of his desk and sized-up the class. He then placed his hands in front of him as he leaned back on his desk.

Richard was so confident in his skin he had a uniquely honest aura about him that you could instinctively feel and experience. You took from Richard the feeling he was a person you could trust. In a journey not yet completed, he seemed a natural guide and leader. One who did not chase after what some of the other teachers would waste time over. Class repartee, class sarcasm, and the pursuit of the superficial mundane concerns of no real importance except to the megalomaniacs who pathologically use the gray areas of life's journey to hide the enviousness and the cowards and the cruelty of their own messed up displaced fears. I began to feel that the school might have something cool to offer because Richard was cool and above the usual ridicule.

I continued to sit while unpacking my books when the head nun walked in and when she left Richard told everyone to form a semi-circle, and everyone began moving to the front of the classroom. The scraping of desks on the floor sounded trumpet-like, only being slightly out of tune and time, unconventional notes filling the room as we moved around. I followed a classmate named Dave with little choice as he took hold of my desk and dragged it along across the room to the most desirable spot in the room that key spot next to Cassie. We ended up near Penny.

Call me Dave, what's your name?" asked Dave.

"Will," I said.

"I like what you did, not standing up for Mother Superior," said Dave. "It's awesome, and I always wanted to do something like that in elementary school, but never did."

The Sun They Called the Moon`

Was I supposed to stand, I wondered to myself?

School uniforms for private schools in the United States vary widely by location and individual school. St. Gregory's Catholic Academy modeled their outfits for girls on a European\Japan naval style. The uniforms had white sleeves attached to a dark powder blue sailor style full collar. The vibrant blue hue collar dropped down in a "V" above the abdomen. The pleated skirt, the collar, and the cuffs matched in the same bright sky blue fabric giving the sailor-style collar and the matching pleated skirt the quality of chatoyant silk in sun light bringing out the stronger hues in the sky blue color of the fabric making the sky blue color fabric look even brighter in the sun.

The pleated skirt hemline was 3-4 inches above the knees. The sailor-style cuffs also had two solid blood red embroidery stitches around the wrist against the vibrant blue color fabric matching the two solid ruby red lines around the edges of the powder blue collar. A less vibrant powder blue t-shirt under the neckline filled in under the "V" of the sky blue sailor-style collar, white horizontal solid stripes connected the "V" going across the top of the t-shirt barely showing the Academy's logo under it. A deep blood red ribbon laced in two loops formed a pretty bow that hung at the bottom of the "V" of the sailor-style collar. The girls wore alternate forms of legwear such as loose socks, but the more fashionable girls with their sailor outfits commonly matched knee-length stockings.

The girls' sports-activity uniform was a basic t-shirt and a bikini bottom overskirt that attached to the waist. Students had been wearing the same style uniforms under the dress code all of their academic lives. Attempts to subvert the dress code by wearing uniforms incorrectly or by adding prohibited elements such as high leg stockings, and wearing unofficial t-shirts under the sky blue sailor-style collar were commonplace, nearly everyday uprisings, as girls would even attempt shortening their skirts.

The boys wore a white dress shirt and a deep red ruby colored tie with a simple two button down sports jacket. The jacket was dark blue to match the uniform pants that oddly blended in with the tie by a tint of ruby red in the blue trousers. The boys' attempts to subvert the

Academy's dress code were more elusive crusades compared to that of the girls' efforts. The boys broke dress code usually by wearing the uniform incorrectly with an open collar. This included no tie or claims of a lost tie, shirt worn outside the waistband and hoisting the sports jacket between the straps of a required blue backpack, never wearing the jacket of course, but always carrying it just in case one needed to put it on in a hurry for the fashion police.

"Doesn't she look like a witch walking around the Academy?" asked Cassie, turning her attractive face quickly, followed by her hair in a three-ply hairstyle flowing across her lively smile and then rebounding back across her face. I noticed she was wearing a bright red bandanna cuffed around her left arm that showed a solid black circle with a red dot in the center. Then I realized why every person was gunning across the room towards her. She was hot. If I noticed her, I would have been dragging Dave across the room instead of him dragging me. Cassie was not unlike their North Star, and they were not unlike the constellations containing her. Cassie did not seem to notice all the attentions, but did she? I had to wonder.

The Sun They Called the Moon`

When I said hello to Hoshimi for the first time she was already next to Cassie and had no need to cover any distance to get to a space near her. Hoshimi was a gracefully slender girl with hair measured out to the nape of her neck wearing noticeably round wheel specs; she studiously sat skimming over a textbook for the next lesson and did not inconvenience herself to look up, but acknowledged me with an unmotivated, "Hi." She was fond of causing emotional disturbances amongst the uniform fascist fashionista's by wearing a sport's blazer she made herself out of a light, velvety material she picked up somewhere that was a million to one color match for the pants the boys were wearing. How she slipped on the blazer was a statement in itself. By wearing the jacket directly under her sailor-style collar that went down over her breasts to her flat stomach in a "V", she argued her jacket was within the Academy's dress code. The fascist fashionistas have not been able to throw an effective counterpunch at her argument, as her blazer is a result of the Academy's "dress code" as written to the letter.

Greg Tarantino and Mike Redwood went flying across from the other side of the room trying to beat Bill and Leo for a spot next to Cassie. Greg and Mike had gotten a good running start and nearly knocked Leo and Bills' desk out the door.

"Machine one," Greg shouted as if he just gained some kind of advantage while Bill and Leo picked-up their desk. "You fat face! You can't stop this rental baby," Greg continued, pointing to his desk.

"That Tarantino, he has to start. This time, Cassie, I'm not going to take it," said Leo, his hands flying in the air, "just wait Tarantino," he warned.

"Ah-ha," Greg replied, pointing to Leos' round head and square rim glasses.

"Hi, Will," said Cassie, exuberantly, giving voice to a pair of eyes that seem to grow at the sound of her voice and made you feel like you were the only person there. "You sure got spunk not standing for her. I always wanted to do that. I tend to get stuck doing stuff like that to prove that an effort can make a difference in changing the way things are to what they can better become, but "that", I never did."

"That's cool," said Leo. "I always wanted to do something like that too, but I never had the opportunity."

"This is so super awesome Will, I always wanted to do something like that, it's like superhero stuff," said Penny, looking up at me, wide-eyed with an uncomplicated eagerness to believe and to please, evoking an independence with blushing naïve simplicity.

"I didn't know about having to stand up. I am new to this school," I said. Then Penny's eyes disappeared into two tight crescent shaped lines as if her eyes had to make way for her smile. All at once, I became aware of how her beautiful hair flowed down her shoulders. It flowed like the melody of a clear flowing stream. Penny had more curves at her disposal than any doctrine of salvation by grace should allow, but there she was in front of me in all her curvy glory. Seeing how easily she blushed, I without the will or conscious control suddenly began to return her blush with my own.

"That's right!" Cassie said as she hammered down the palm of her hand that made Penny and I jump. "You're our new mystery story student. You must have a story. Why would someone transfer in the middle of a school year? Huh?"

"This is Cassie, Janie, and Hoshimi and this is-" said Penny, in sweet hi tones that seemed to chirp out the words delightfully from her voice, but slowly. The girl's voice is amazing. I can't believe it, I thought. I died and went to heaven, surrounded by incredibly stacked round bosoms all around me. I sat there and sighed after seeing enough to know I had arrived.

"Penny, I already went through that with him," said Cassie, cutting off Penny in mid-sentence, sternly in a deadpan voice with a glowering scowl on her face. It was as if Cassie had a switch inside her that went from perky and smiley to prickly and bossy. How can anybody be mean to a girl as sweet as Penny? I thought. "You're going to play class sports with us, aren't you? You are athletic aren't you?" continued Cassie, with one eye winked and shut tight, the other piercing at me, and with one accusing pointing index finger in my face demanding the answer.

"Yeah, if you want me to," I quickly answered, as she stood over me. She would have likely ripped my head off if I didn't say yes to her. I heard Penny mewl, letting out a soft, ethereal sound of approval. I turned to see her blushing, again. Then I involuntary returned her blush with my own. Our eyes met, making her face go into a deeper shade of red. She looked down away from me as if to control it.

"I'm telling you with him on our side, we'll take the B class in every game for the rest of the year," declared Cassie. She was acting as if she were an agent for the Yankees, who just acquired a good ball player.

"He's not a small person," said Janie." I think we can take it to class B. We'll have another decent athlete in class A for sure."

"Look at him; He's a good size. He can help us win every game from now on," said Dave, leaning forward and pointing behind him at me with his thumb.

It was soon time to go to lunch. I was looking forward to it and thought lunch was a good time for me to become better acquainted with my new classmates. The lunch line was so long we had to wait in line at the other end of the hall. St. Gregory's Catholic Academy gave you a full hot meal. I didn't mind waiting in line for it. The hot lunch seemed like a good deal. Usually, hot lunch meant hunting hamburger hidden deep within the main course, but today it was a slice of turkey with brown gravy, bright green peas and a piece of chocolate cake.

We all didn't go for the school's hot lunch. Cassie, Hoshimi, Penny, and Janie made their lunch and brought it to school from home. It meant they didn't have to waste time waiting in a long line to eat. It gave them a better-situated place to talk. It gave Cassie more time to plan a strategy for upcoming class activities with them. Something she enjoyed doing.

Gym class and lunch always followed one another at the Academy. This is done by design to throw a bunch of kids struggling to form their identity, gladiator style into athletic competitions to test their moral qualities collectively, primarily distinguishing, and nurturing those qualities.

I saw Cassie from the corner of my eye while I was waiting in line to eat. She liked winning and going for broke. It was obvious to me.

The cafeteria was a good size and one of the several separate buildings on the campus that included the elementary building, junior high building, and the building for the high school. The cafeteria design is intentionally larger. The cafeteria was large enough to accommodate and feed the entire student body at one seating. It at times is asked for by the town to double as an indoor town square for people to meet in the intemperate New England winter months.

The cafeteria was made up of wall-to-wall bricks like the classrooms, only painted blue. The cafeteria had an adjoining room where lay teachers and Sisters who were not on lunch duty that week could eat in privacy without interruptions. The cafeteria had smaller round tables instead of great big long lecture style ones that faced front in one direction. The round table seating is one of Richard's ideas and was not one that Mother Superior wanted to see happen.

It meant that she and other teachers could no longer oppressively stand and stare in front of students while they ate. Teachers and nuns now had to walk in between and around tables in the cafeteria. Richard found it ironic that some teachers who demanded that students show respect by standing every time they walked into a classroom did not feel they should have to exert themselves to show those same students respect back when they were eating. For the Academy's students, it meant they could eat without having to look up and see their teachers staring back at them. They could eat in peace.

All the teachers had to walk a patrol in an assigned area within the cafeteria during their lunch duty. It was a new policy put in place by Mother Superior. But it was payback for Richard leading other teachers who agreed with him to the PTA, overturning Mother Superior's rejection of the round tables and getting the change implemented.

Richard enjoyed sitting down with students at any time, but especially during lunchtime. So did Sister Carolyn and Sister Christine, but every time Mother Superior would walk in they would all have to get up. All it took was a grave penetrating look from Mother Superior to them, and they all got up to walk to their assigned cafeteria areas for watching, repressing, protecting, and inspecting. Every once in a while Sister Christine found some students she could yell at for a disciplinary reason, which seemed to reassure Mother Superior that discipline of students in the cafeteria of St. Gregory's Catholic Academy was enforced and rules followed.

However, once Mother Superior left, Richard, Sister Carolyn, and Sister Christine made their way back to sitting and laughing with students.

I finally sat down to lunch with Greg Tarantino, Mike Redwood, Bill, Leo, and Dave. Just a table or two away from Cassie, Hoshimi, Penny, and

Janie who were about done with their lunch when I noticed how in sync they all were with their hair styles. Although their hair varied in length and colors their hairs had the same texture but with varying straight cuts and angles giving each one of them an original hairstyle with an original sharp look.

They all sat with their sylphlike legs exceptionally visible and folded up under their light blue skirts as they were talking and laughing with one another. They were clearly redesigning new game plans for the upcoming sports competitions. I heard Cassie quickly rattling off the future playing orders to indoor soccer, track and field contests with excitement. Cassie had an ability to pass quickly to Hoshimi, Penny, and Janie her can do mental attitude.

Meanwhile, I took a bite of what I believed was turkey or fake turkey, knowing the food of the day was a real toss-up because no one could answer for me for sure what they bought, turkey, fake turkey, or what we were eating that day. "The girls around here are really into athletic competition," I said.

"Da, ya think, look around, we devour it. Wait until you see this place at Science Fair, Harvest Festival, and Drama Festival time," said Mike Redwood.

"You should know class activities are what this Academy's about," said Dave.

"But, the rest of the schools think we are a band of flakes, led by the Academy's biggest snow queen, Cassie," said Greg Tarantino. "Cassie will go out on a date with a guy if she's asked, but she keeps a strict one-date rule with every guy she dates, leaving the guy barking at the moon for more."

"Lots of guys think she's a tease, but it's her way and her rule. They don't know her the way we do," said Leo.

"We are lucky we got to know her in class, but we're just as dead to her like any other guy in school," said Dave, reaching for a bottle of water.

"I'd give anything to spend five minutes with Miss Jug Fest," added Greg Tarantino with an appreciative gleefulness in his voice.

She's a buy one get one free booby sandwich," said Mike Redwood, lost somewhere in the stratosphere of his mind. "I could have knockers like hers every day for the rest of my life."

I couldn't settle for just one set to play with. Penny is the real booby girl with a milk mouth. She has one grade-A-rack, hanging those things out to dry in front of my face. God, they are so hot. I want to squeeze and nipple her," said Greg Tarantino.

"You two have tits on the brain," replied Leo.

"Oh yeah, tell me about it. Last spring when Hoshimi was at shortstop with those long slender legs of hers that go on and on forever, Leo, you didn't dive bomb her on purpose from center field while running after a fly ball? She landed right on top of you. Tell me you didn't like her shoving her milk sacks in your face," said Greg Tarantino. "You were down there with her long enough to name each one of her cans."

"The school's Soccer Olympic Finals are the best," Bill declared, as if it was a non-debatable statistical certainty, judging the best games upon bounciness. Janie has the pair of cans I'd like to name. She runs so hard with those supple melons, flopping around, and hitting her in the face; I swear she is going to burst a lip on those nicely firm cans of hers someday. I can't stop looking at her fun bags. I could pet those Chihuahuas a thousand times. They are the knocker-boobs of all time."

"She's going to crack you in the nuts," said Dave. "Put a pair of breasts in front of these guys, and they can't tell them from their face, but no matter how juicy the rack you can't beat Cassie's smoking tight-ass. It's perfect"

Cassie, Hoshimi, Penny, and Janie, who had been unusually silent and sitting near us, picked up their backpacks and left their table. Why these guys couldn't figure out there was a difference in telling a girl, I can't resist your puppy dog eyes, from I can't resist your puppies, I'll never know. But Cassie, Hoshimi, Penny, and Janie all had detectable smirks on their faces. "Hey, girls", they all said, smiling, walking passed us to change for P.E.

"Oh, by the way, Greg, we reposition the team, and we're going to try Will at your spot," Cassie said, looking over her shoulder.

"But I thought I was the goalie," said Greg Tarantino.

"We thought we might vomit on you, instead of keeping you as a goalie. But since we thought you might like it, we changed our minds," said Janie, without troubling herself to turn around as they pushed through the cafeteria double doors.

"What's their problem, really?" said Leo.

Chapter 9

Sister Moon

Richard walked over to Sister Carolyn and Sister Christine standing in the cafeteria after Mother Superior walked back to her office. "So how is the new student doing? I can't imagine what it must be like for a transferee from a public school to transfer into a private Academy like this one and in the middle of a semester," said Sister Carolyn. "How far behind is your new transferee?"

"He's not, Will is ahead in the class," said Richard. "Will seems to be a little more mature than the other boys in the class, and he's a good kid."

Sister Carolyn adjusted her nun cap covering the top, back, and sides of her head. Richard watched as her hair came down in a blonde side bang that floated across her brow and rested there. Before he caught up with himself, he was staring into her green eyes. They were warm and quiet, gentler than a cheerful smile. As she noticed him looking at her, a degree of warmth filled her with a quality yielding to a comfortable affection, but it did not hide the instinctive over familiarity hanging in the air during the exchange of enthusiasm, excitement, and a sudden parting glance of tender confidence.

"What are you two doing?" said Sister Christine, bluntly. She placed her two hands firmly on her side.

"What do you mean? What are you saying?" replied Richard, hesitating before saying and forgetting what he was going to say.

"Are you heading back to class?" asked Sister Christine, calmly, in an apparent attempt to lead them back to earth, swaying on her toes and heels, waiting, tight-lipped for any commonsensical response.

"No, no, I'll push the stragglers into the locker rooms," said Richard, finally.

Sister Christine in exasperation grabbed Sister Carolyn's arm. "We need to have a long talk, again," said Sister Christine, in a huff and led Sister Carolyn off to the girl's locker room.

Sister Carolyn was born Carolyn Somers. She was the only child of actor Bernie Somers and Harriett Hicks who married when they were 16 and 17. Both were beautiful people, and Somers always expresses extreme admiration for them. They separated and ultimately divorced when she was a teenager. As an only child, she was not raised Catholic but was converted to the religion when Carolyn was 12. She lived in Chicago with her grandparents, who insisted she go to the parochial school, not for its religious education but because it was the neighborhood school. She once told Richard, "As a child I was sharp. My parents married when they were 16 and 17, and both were beautiful people. They had movie offers, so we moved from Chicago to Hollywood. I was a Hollywood holy terror. We lived in Beverly Hills, and I used to visit the studio lots with my parents." Somers' is also blood-related by marriage, through an aunt, to the actor, Spenser Tracy.

In Beverly Hills, as a teenager, after her parents divorced, she had lived with her mother, who married a restaurant owner. Somers studied at UCLA, before entering the convent at St. Gregory Catholic Academy. While studying as an underclassman, she was once engaged to a scientist that taught at her college, but that lasted for a few semesters until he replaced her with a newer girl wonder from one of his classes. She was no stranger to being attractive. Even stripped of all makeup, her appearance tapped into that question as to why she would reject it all and so completely to be the bride of Christ.

The spiritual focus, of the Carmelite Order, is contemplative prayer. The Order is by the Church to be under the special protection of the Blessed Virgin Mary and thus has a strong Marian devotion. As in most of the orders dating to medieval times, the First Order is the Friars. The Second Order are the nuns (who are cloistered) and the Third Order in which she first participated consisted of seculars who continue to live in the world but participate in the charism of the order by liturgical prayers, apostolate, and contemplative prayer. The Carmelite Order jumped out to her as a natural development in the direction of becoming an active Carmelite sister, so she joined the Carmelite Monastery in San Diego, CA.

"Do you know? Do you know that this is what you have been searching for and have found with us?" asked the Prioress at the Benedictine Abbey.

"Yes," said Somers. "The picture of Heaven and eternity grow more convincing to me over time. I examine my heart, and I can see it."

"Yes, the big picture is what we need to keep an eye on," said the Mother, the Prioress. "Let us see if a transformation of both our impressions can at last occur. You have been sensing there are times you may not be so sure haven't you?"

"At times," said Somers, "but I can sense the presence of an animating force and being transported beyond myself. This feeling of liberation far exceeds anything I ever dreamed of or hoped in the freedom of a personal relationship with Christ."

"But Sometimes," said the Prioress.

"Yes," said Somers.

"It is because you still will not have the instruments of separation reinterpreted as means for salvation, and used for purposes of love?" asked, the Prioress.

"What do you mean?" asked Somers.

"Everyone has experienced what you call a sense of being transported beyond themselves at one time or another. This feeling of liberation far exceeds the sense of freedom sometimes hoped for and by most even imagined. It is a sensation of real escape from temporal limitations. If you consider what this "transportation" really means, you will recognize that it is an immediate unawareness of the body and a joining of yourself to something in which your mind enlarges to encompass it," said the Prioress.

"We can make fantasies in which our will conflicts with His. Do you understand me? Good, fantasies have made your body your enemy; weak, vulnerable and treacherous, worthy of the hate that you invest in it. This serves you not in your time with us. You have identified with a thing you hate, the instrument of vengeance, and the sensed source of your guilt. But you have done this to something that has no true meaning, proclaiming it to be the space of God's Son, and turning it against him. Are you still with me?" asked the Prioress.

"I think, Mother Superior," said Somers.

"Your body cannot limit you, merely because you would have it so because you were not really "lifted out" of it; it cannot restrain you at all. You go where you must always be, gaining, not losing His presence. In these instants of release from physical restrictions, we experience much of what happens in a spiritual space. The lifting of the obstructers of time and space, the impromptu experience of peace and joy, and, above all, the back and forth awareness of the body which questions us to whether or not all this is possible.

However, it is only possible when you decide you want it. The sudden expansion of consciousness takes place with your desire for it. The Holy Spirit holds this irresistible appeal. He calls to you to be yourself, within his safe embrace. They are the laws of limits lifted for you by Him to welcome you to the openness of mind and freedom. He attracts our attention in this way to summon us all to a space of refuge, where we can be ourselves in peace. Peace joins us there, simply because we have let go the limits we have placed upon love and joined it where it is and where it led us, in answer to the call to be at peace," said the Prioress.

"I understand," said Somers.

"Do you my dear? You still have too much faith in the body as your source of strength. What plans do you make that do not involve persistently slipping out of the Abby and your mind, reluctantly perhaps not fully recognizing it, all for your comfort, protection, or enjoyment in some way? This makes the body an end and not a means in your journey with us, and this always means you still find this other way of life more attractive to you. No one accepts this life for herself who still accepts these attractions as their goal. Thus, you have not met your responsibility," said the Prioress.

"But I have Holy Mother," said Somers, fearing she would be let go.

I am not judging you, but I find myself looking at and envying what God has in store for you," said the Prioress.

"You envy me, but why Sister?" asked Somers.

"Should it not, then, be that you would still call on love to enter? Love knows no bodies and strains to everyone without exception being created like it. Love's total lack of limit is its meaning. It is impartial in its giving, embracing only to preserve and to keep complete what it would give.

The body does not know. A tiny kingdom has so little, so should it not, then, be that some would call on love to enter and not find it? And while they limit their awareness to the self-inflation of its tiny senses, they will not see the grandeur that surrounds them. God cannot come into a body, nor can they join Him there. The limits on love will always seem to shut Him out and keep them separate from Him. The body is a tiny fence around a little part of a brilliant and complete idea. It draws a circle, infinitely small, around a very microscopic part of Heaven, splintering it from the whole, maintaining that within it is the Kingdom of God, but where God cannot enter. Can you see the unavailing dry, desolate, and joyless scorched desert that makes up that little kingdom?" asked the Prioress.

"Yes," Mother, it is why I am here," said Somers.

"Ah," said the Prioress slapping her palm to the chair as if to say, there it is, knowing Somers was in between two conflicting forces and knowing you cannot retreat from the world if you fear it. Because being afraid you must then believe the fear and are joined to that world by what you believe.

"What a strange position must it be for those in a world who must carry a tremendous organic counterweight of themselves, stumbling through their life trying to feel with their eyes, but never within? Each is a body that seems to house a separate mind, a disconnected thought, enduring alone and in no way connected to the thought by which it is created. Each tiny fragment seeming to be self-contained, needing another for some things, but by no means entirely and consistently connected to its one Creator for everything; requiring the whole to give it purpose not knowing by itself, it means nothing. Nor does it have any life apart and by itself.

Oh, and they have the nerve to say we are the ones who are cloistered?" said the Prioress.

"So then can I continue to stay with the Sisters at the Abbey?" asked Somers.

"You are with us every time you realize the life and joy that love would bring to you from where it comes, and where it would return with you, Sister. You can stay until the day you are unable," said the Prioress.

It did not baffle Sister Carolyn when Richard looks at her steadily and intently, especially, in admiration, in surprise, unembarrassed and without shame in front the world. She felt the noncommittal part of her becoming whole and began to form at first what was a much interfered with an emotional bond with Richard that grew with the emotional intelligence giving her an ability to perceive and assess the emotions of herself and others for the first time in a long time.

Sister Carolyn in return found her feelings for Richard equally as unworldly as her being sent out to a way of living to which one lends oneself to God to his service in particular work or a unique position, or to a state of salvation. Sister

The Sun They Called the Moon`

Carolyn's growing social relationship with Richard remained a problem for most of the nuns in the convent next door to the Academy until Father Vincent who was President of St. Gregory's Catholic Academy said it was not a problem and then it was not as if he willed it on to them.

Chapter 10

Flowers that Bloom between the Earth and the Moon

Sunshine does not bother you on a spring morning. It spoils you. On the first spring morning of that year, rays of sunshine played on my eyelids. I lifted out of my bed awakened by a warm, radiant halcyon stream flowing into the room, sweeping up every curiosity within its reach.

It took me only a few steps towards the windowpane to feel the difference in my atmosphere. I flung open the windows of my room to feel the fresh spring air and to get a better view of the open green meadows that were gentle and soothing. It was a beautiful spring morning with the sweet smell of Magnolias bursting into flowers. Fields interspersed by colorful beds of tulips and roses, red, white, pink, yellow, truly, a sight to be treasured. High-pitched sounds of birds filled my ears, and multi-colored efflorescence greeted my eyes. When the earth finally casts off its morose wintry blanket and as the flowers begin to blossom, so does one's irrefutable liveliness. When every deserving soul welcomes the season's open arms, the sense of lavishness and plenteousness of the green gardens fills every true heart as the freshly minted sunshine thaws out the edges of any despair.

I stepped out of my house and took it all in with a deep breath. I went into this captivating beauty and its blooms to feel the breeze, watch the fluttering butterflies, and spot the hummingbirds, in a fading attempt to appreciate, and capture the moment in my mind's eye. The air smelled earthy, and the pendulous sleeping plants were now floating at attention in their newfound youth beguiling me in their unusual lightness and delicacy in their living web of irrepressibility. Rays of sunlight shimmered through the dewdrops and slid down the blades of the breezy green grass. I walked to my bike to leave for school.

The Sun They Called the Moon`

I peddled down the hill to race out along the road that seemed to melt down in front of me like a dancer stretched out, bowing down impressively along the sea. I felt the beautiful wet texture of sea mist fall on my face. I took the full scent of the fresh sea air into me. The morning was filling up with the hustle, bustle, and commotion of both the hearty and the young-at-heart. A Sparrow nudging its tiny head around focused on the sound of my bike chain slipping out of gear, bound to the first glimpses of the season's triumphant cheer, starts to follow me, quickly flying out of there.

The springtime of the year is the best-loved season for many people, and it is easy to understand why this might be so. The ability of spring with its natural regenerative effects freshly reinterprets the condition of renewing in every major holiday that includes every major religion in the spring season. From Passover to Easter, it seems that every culture claims spring with a celebration of renewal and new life. It is easy to understand how and why the power of spring and the beauty of new life gladden both the heart and civilization alike.

The Sun They Called the Moon`

I dashed into the small parking bike area of the Academy that rapidly began filling up with bikes arriving all at once and with not much time left to spare in one motion; I was off up the stair. Cassie turned her head around as she walked in front of me. My eyes were level with the back of her legs. My eyeballs followed the invisible line of her socks all the way up her thighs. There were barely three inches of skin before the hem of her bright sky-blue skirt caught the sun. When her shining gossamer blue skirt suddenly caught the wind her skirt easily floated up above the color of the pale flesh moons of her crescent shaped curves Carved and divided in two with a firmness of a sweet peach occupying, and gently pushing out from under the opposite sides of the white panty lines above her legs. Cassie moved up the staircase like a walking poem.

"Good morning, it's so nice to see you again," she said with a smile that made the muscles of her upper face rise enough for her eyes to squint at me. I smiled back as I felt the hairs on the back of my neck heat up as I lit up all inside.

The Sun They Called the Moon`

"I am so going to win this guy," said Cassie, after she turned to run off and away.

Later in the day, I found myself skipping lunch to get in some last-minute cramming before a test that was going to be happening in my next class. It was the first time I had a test at St. Gregory Catholic Academy in the afternoon. My problem was not so much reviewing for an exam, but finding a space somewhere in St. Gregory Catholic Academy to sit down and study, St. Gregory Catholic Academy the number one competitive school on the planet.

I finally discovered one room that was empty at lunchtime. Being still relatively new, it took a few tries to find one distinct, but empty room. I went in, sat down at one of the desks, began to study intensely not too aware of, and not too concerned about what was happening outside the room.

Well, in my defense, the room wasn't marked by any easy to see sign. That would have been nice when I think back on it. But then again I would not be witness to one of the most awe-inspiring and extraordinary things that I ever witnessed in person with my own eyes. I didn't know that such a fabulous surprise was humanly possible in my mind-numbing life.

But then again, maybe I should not have been so quick to be so smart and stopped to realize every school had this one distinct room and figured out I was sitting in it.

After all, folks pay school taxes, right. They sometimes have slackers that must go to school, right? To try to learn something so (hopefully) they won't become a burden on society, right? Should their parents try to step in they will simply be suspended or thrown out of school entirely and have to go to a public school, right?

Where did the thought come from that necessitates a behavior modification room for learning, when did external operant conditioning come to modify and control the something said or regarded to be; genuine behavior of people? Who is doing this external operant conditioning today and who do they think they are.

Every secondary, junior high, high school or elementary school distributes a handbook for prescribed patterns of behavior, including St. Gregory Catholic Academy. A book, which I did not at the time read. It is a "rule book" to students, and each student by law in the school district must receive one. If you don't have one, you should have no trouble obtaining one. Read it. Know what it states because it will tell you your "rights."

In some instances, a parent must be involved in the process. Your handbook will tell you how that works, too. Finally, if you have a documented statement from a parent or guardian, then you stand a better chance of substantiating your claim of "innocence." I hope this helps answer the question for the record on how I ended up in the school's detention room without realizing it.

Written Rules for detention for St. Gregory's Catholic Academy state that no student is allowed into detention without his or her current year issued SGCA school picture ID. Furthermore, failure to comply with the limits in the book of rules will result in a discipline report sent to the principal, and further disciplinary action will be taken. If a student does not have current papers, he/she may obtain it from the bookstore (a converted closet) before 1:00 P.M. and after 3:00 P.M. If a student does not have $10.00, it will be a charge to their student account. Students report to Room B-73. The same Room B-73 I am fervently studying in for my afternoon exam.

After school, daily detention begins as follows:

3:50 P.M. to 5:15 P.M. or 1:50 P.M. to 3:15 P.M.

NO EXCEPTIONS

2. After school, double detention is on Thursdays only for the time beginning at 3:50 P.M. sharp ending at 6:35 P.M. double detentions are also on Tuesdays only for the time beginning at 1:50 P.M. sharp ending at 4:35 P.M.

NO EXCEPTIONS

3. The student is required to take all coats, books, etc. to the detention room-he/ she is not allowed to go to their locker after detention.

4. The student must bring homework to complete.

5. Card playing, games, radios/cassettes/headphones, etc. are not allowed.

6. Talking is not permitted.

7. The student is not permitted to sleep or assume a sleeping position.

8. The student is not allowed to leave the Detention Room without Supervisor's permission.

9. Assigned after school daily/double detention time missed due to suspension, or student absence requires the student to immediately

complete their punishment upon the return to school.

Students waiting for the 5:20/6:55 P.M. activity bus must report directly to the Cafeteria - all other students should have prearranged transportation needs made. Students must leave the building as soon as possible. No loitering is allowed.

PLEASE NOTE: "Student not complying with the After School Daily/Double Detention rules or do not serve an assigned detention is subject to additional disciplinary action as stated in accordance with the Parent Student Handbook, which is another book of rules."

School discipline is a system of rules, punishments, and behavioral modification strategies appropriate to the regulation of children and the maintenance of order in the school by the school and for the school. Its aim is to control the student's actions and behavior. An obedient student is a good student and complies with the school rules and codes of conduct. These rules may, for example, define the expected standards of clothing, timekeeping, social behavior, and work ethic. The term discipline applies to the punishment that is the consequence of breaking the rules of behavior. The aim of discipline is to set limits restricting certain behaviors pointed out or declared harmful. The aptitude or talent to declare harmful something by which restricting behavior is activated, the discernments, and most reasons for it I never did get.

Well, if you are still with me, do you remember not too many pages back I mentioned there are attempts to subvert the dress code by wearing uniforms incorrectly. The above reference rulebook, for example, defines the expected standards of "clothing."

There is a natural human desire to give into the instinctive self-actualization of one's human personal identity and dignity in attempts to turn away from years of dictated conformity. You may want to keep that in mind for a little later.

There are only about three known public theories based on expert opinions about school discipline practices. A school's discipline practices come by way of some knowledgeable educators and by the theories from behavioral psychologists called, Skinnerian's, followers of the theories of operant conditioning in which an individual's behavior is modified by enforcing outside consequences that are outside the person's comprehension and control. The science is a fact, has been around for many years in and around our lives, and has been built upon, modified and expanded. It is unbound and unrestrained in both closed and opened civilize territories to determine and control all sorts of human behavior.

B.F. Skinner is benignly recognized as the father of modern marketing and advertising. While experimenting with birds and some homemade feeding controllers; Skinner invented the operant conditioning chamber (A box) which allowed him to measure rates of responses as a key dependent variable using a cumulative record of lever presses or key pecks. The theories are in use in some form or other all around us. The science of behavior modification has evolved in its capacity to have an effect on character, development, and behavior.

The Sun They Called the Moon`

Behavior modifications have had the power to shape policy through the study of patterns of behavior.

There is enough public corroborated theories of mass behavior modification to form a comprehensive discipline strategy for an entire school or a particular class, but the three main ones are as follows:

The Positive Approach

The Positive Approach is established in the teachers' esteem for the students. Instilling in their students a sense of duty by connecting youth to adult tie-ins to develop and apply clear rules for providing daily chances for success, and administering in-school suspension for noncompliant students. Based on Glasser's Reality Therapy, Research (e.g., Allen) is supportive of the PAD program.

Teacher Effectiveness Training

Teacher Effectiveness Training distinguishes between teacher-possessed and student-conceded problems and proposes different strategies for dealing with each. Students are taught problem-solving and negotiation techniques. Researchers (e.g., Emmer and Aussiker) find that teachers like this program and that their behavior is influenced by it, although effects on student responses are unclear.

And The Adlerian Approach

The Adlerian Approach is a comprehensive term for an assortment of methods that emphasize understanding the individual's reasons for maladjusted behavior and helping misbehaving students to alter their behavior, while at the same time finding ways to get their needs met. Presumably, assuming the student's misbehavior was not because their needs were not being met, but because their teachers were too busy with theories from experts. Named for psychiatrist Alfred Adler, these approaches have shown some positive effects on self-concept, attitudes, and zone control.

We may also suspect the thoughts John B. Watson, Edward Thorndike and later B.F. Skinner that brought the operant conditioning chambers and skilled scientific procedure of operant conditioning here and why it is around and still unbound. The Rulebook says you must give an affirmative reply to an obiter dictum; say yes to detention without question. Whether you think you deserve it or not, you must accept the fact and deal with it. Do not assume or assert you are right and that the teacher/sister or authority who gave you the detention is incorrect. Make a note of the time and room number and whom the detention is with for example a special detention supervisor, a teacher or even the watchful eye of the Mother Superior or Sister or head abrogator.

Note if it is a break time, lunchtime or after school detention and whether it is in a classroom, a hall or in a different building. Make sure you know what you will be doing for punishment. Check the rubbish collection schedule before going. You may be required to clean under the desks (especially if you were caught chewing gum in school) during detention time. In that case, do not wear clean clothes or shoes, and expect to get dirty.

You will handwrite lines in accordance with what you did to get the detention; i.e. "I must arrive on time to all my lessons." If you finish early, expect to sit down and read or do homework in the allocated time. Do not communicate with others in any way. You will not leave detention early.

You need to make traveling plans. If you catch a bus, make sure you know whether there is another bus, or whether you will have to walk home. Ask your parents to pick you up, or have enough money; you will have to take a taxi. If there is no available transportation, you will have to ask your parents or guardians to write or telephone the school as to changing the time, i.e. if an after-school detention can be changed to Saturday detention. You should be the one to check that, and you should do it before the day is over the day before detention. Be reasonable and accept that if you live close by and go home by walking, you are unlikely to be allowed to change an after-school detention to a Saturday one.

Arrive on time. Just because you think you did not do anything wrong, you cannot turn up late. Arriving on time presents a confident person, and can make people less likely to handing you more detention. Present yourself well. Wear your school uniform. Wear it proudly and correctly, i.e. with the tie or ribbon done up properly, shirt tucked in and skirted properly directed with no extra add-ons like foul-smelling belts or badges. If you have to wear foul-smelling belts, or badges, keep them in your backpack and put them on after the detention. Hitch up the trousers, pull down the skirts to a reasonable length and just grin and bear it. As soon as you step off the school property, you can put your uniforms back to how you like them.

Do not repeat what you did to get the detention in the detention room. If you got the detention for being late to a class, arrive on time for detention. If you got the detention for carrying contraband or wearing your uniform incorrectly, do not wear them incorrectly or hide add-on device/buttons/badges/belts in detention. Indeed, taking your belt off for that amount of time will not kill you. Do not chew gum. It is a sure way to get more detention.

The Sun They Called the Moon`

Do what the teacher tells you i.e. where to sit. Do not argue or ignore them. Be polite, and calm in the detention. Do not speak out loudly to proclaim your innocence or how unfair is the detention. It is a sure fire way of getting more detention. It is not in your best interests to do so.

Thus, "Spoke" the Rules for Detention for St. Gregory's Catholic Academy with theories from trained psychologists and expert educators.

However, the rules as written did seem more along the ideas of German philosophers Georg Wilhelm Friedrich Hegel, Bruno Bauer, and Friedrich Nietzsche than what Jesus taught.

More along the ideas of the Übermensch, the veiled ideas of Nietzsche's notions, the suspect thoughts that brought us here are of "self-mastery," "self-cultivation," "self-direction," and "self-overcoming," "I teach you the Overman is something that shall be overcome. What have you done to overcome him? All beings so far have created something beyond themselves; and do you want to be the ebb of this great flood and even go back to the beasts rather than overcome man?

What is the ape to man?

A laughingstock or a painful embarrassment and man shall be just that for the Overman: a laughingstock or a painful embarrassment. You have made your way from worm to man, and much in you is still worm. Once you were apes, and even now, too, man is more ape than any ape..." - Thus Spoke Zarathustra, Prologue, §three, Trans.

A German philosopher says, "Man is more ape than any ape," and the idea becomes a trumpet that never triumphs, calling for the gathering of deceptions by the exalted to join and rejoice with their drunk on privilege masters. How they hardened at the sound of the insane illusion of everyone's littleness, except their own. They cannot return pride because pride cannot share and do not return love because love must be share.

The Sun They Called the Moon`

The names of people and places may change through the chronicle of time, but the results of insane ideas will always be insane. As those of whose feet travel on this ancient road will always run to the ancient evil that makes haste to shed the blood of the innocent so that this planet shall become the desolation. These insane ideas were never true inside or outside Eden or even history. What the belief in the exceptionality of the Overman produced was sorrow and depression, sickness and pain, darkness and dark imaginings of terror, cold fantasies of fear and fiery furnaces of hell.

All the same, does not it at least beg the question; how can an authoritative assertion that humanity is profane emerge as profound in a sane mind? Can the answer be as logical and as simple as the fact that insanity cannot reside in a healthy mind and from that fact conclude it must only happen in a sick mind compelled into irrationality by repeated attempts to make what is not real reality?

Did the constant shaking to otherwise healthy minds force them to create an unreality to make it yield to an outside will for that other wills control to maximize profit finally break our brain or has this mental meddling given way to more harmful and evil uses?

No way, right, we are much too smart to be lab rats trapped in a psychological box, manipulated by patterns of outside influence that we can hardly understand or control. Too intelligent to be affected by scientifically proven behavioral patterns that are hand plucked by people who study this most studied modern science for the purpose of mass manipulation of their people. It cannot happen and will not work, here you say.

Nevertheless, we all heard of Sigmund Freud and perhaps Carl Young in the context of a quick gag, a joke, which might discredit the whole notion of psychoanalysis and behavioral theory as something of a trick done to citizens who believe something went wrong in their mind.

We keep on laughing. It is so "hilarious" the science that affects our everyday lives. No one thinks of laughing at their freedom when they are in a war, no one thinks of laughing at their liberty when a company or government takes their livelihood away with a layoff notice, and no one thinks of laughing at their freedom when they lose everything and don't know why.

We would never think of laughing at cancer, but we can laugh here at this growing evolving science, even allow ourselves to be encouraged to laugh at this emerging science through the circles of mass communication, which is the vehicle of this science. We almost never connect this important emerging science to the Ad men of Madison Avenue or Wall Street to the control of a government(s) or by the government(s), oh, freedom can be funny and so sidesplitting, "hilarious."

Consider the device you are holding in your hand. How do you know that it is real? If the instrument were a disavowed or not openly acknowledged or displayed, but concealed technology, you would not know if it were real. It would give you feedback, an instance of visual perception that is all. You would not know its purpose and therefore, not know it is real. The justification of the act of the belief that it is real comes from people that are distinct from that, which is not real who collectively recognize it as being real.

However, if you wish to create a mass delusion and make the illusion look real you simply reverse it. You systematically plant the illusion as real in the population and release it in a guerrilla force. The tipping point rule is the greater the mass delusion, the more guerrillas you need to make it real in the collective mind of the population.

Doctrines of denial to inalienable human rights are not innate. Racism, bigotry, and intolerance must be carefully cultivated and what is inborn must be untaught. Doctrines of personal identity denial are rooted in dogmatism, fanaticism, chauvinism, jingoism, sectarianism, racialism, sexism. What an intolerable strain for humanity to pass on repeatedly the ancient past by refusing to give faith to what has always been true, and to see reality.

The continued inner denial of the common distinctive nature of all individual people through all differences as testified to by the self-awareness, is rooted in the insane belief in the exceptionality of the Overman and is from a space belonging to a more primitive past than our own. I use the name, the Overman, but the names are legion because they are a substitution of a lie for the truth. This idea has been so splintered and subdivided again and again, over and over, that it is now almost impossible to perceive it once was and still is the belief in a delusion.

A lie that was so vast and so utterly incredible that from it a world of total unreality had to emerge. Moreover, is it that strange that the world in which everything is backward and upside down comes out of it?

A space born from a primal fear that the earth is haphazardly slapped together to be hell is presented within the attractive edges of existential nihilism, which argues that life is without objective meaning, purpose, or intrinsic value until some future time or not at all. It always must tempt withdrawal from the present moment least you find the solution to the problem where it exists. The alien and strange manifestation of loathing the sentiments of human pity, care, tolerance, and mercy for what is unique in its diversity and created the same in its likeness is human-made and is always at the center of humanity's greatest mistakes.

A part of Nietzsche's conservative thought must slip seamlessly and gradually into the weaken mind but, not the superior mind because it must enter the mind that is afraid. Being always afraid, it is ripe for teachings that men are not brothers because this mind is always afraid of others. It fears and scorns the spirit of revolution sincerely, but most of its hatred is for the rebel. It rip-offs a few messianic symbols to create the overman. The overman is the answer of the too powerful but is also a signal telling you when they have become too powerful and have gone insane. They always arrive at these ideas as a point of assembly in history to enter into the world once again. However, first, they must assemble to rationalize their feeble excuse for the loathing in particular of Christian values as well as the divinity of the human spirit for its capacity for good over evil and that, which bound them to be a creature of earth.

By the spring of that year, I had not read their rulebook. Greg Tarantino, Mike Redwood, Bill, Leo, and Dave did not know it. Cassie, Hoshimi,

Penny, and Janie did not bother to read it either as it felt like it was from some foreign world. A strange space, a twisted world far from minds, which are uncluttered and clear yet, a mind created so powerful as to have the ability to learn how in time to hide from itself and betray its uniqueness in the universe by not recognizing or considering it in another.

All doctrines that deny personal identity are the same in this. They need the repetitive cognitive conditioning of repeated teachings of intricate, obvious intercommunicated lies to smother out the truth to choose faith in the Overman. However, there must first be a belief in substitution for substitution is the strongest defense the Overman has for its separation from humanity because it must substitute the names and places to hide from history. Then the speaking for the Overman can begin anew as its followers once again march in the new name of cruelty in the new name of lies and mendacity to return humanity to the endless historical loops that repeat its greatest mistakes.

The mind must be taught slowly that its will is not its own, its thoughts do not belong to itself, and even that it is someone or something else. Why events of historically mistaken identity continue to have the power of Legion placed at the forefront of its private armies and hide the true star we are hard wired to follow because the star is who we are is the stuff of legend.

We all sensed the heavy ill spirit of an anti-presents hovering in the air around us. We sensed its horrible cold dark space, but we did not know its name.

Everything the overman comes to it separates as its sponsors destroy, but the one emotion which separation is impossible is love for love involves not separation by its definition, for fear is separation's substitution for love and both cannot occupy the same place in time and space. One space unites us. The other separates us.

We played, laughed, and love in what was an instant of sunlight in a moment of eternity. The instant is where we all live. It is what we all consume. It is what we all extend through time into eternity, passed the world's ugliness. To a world of beauty, that mesmerizes, never failing in its awe at its perfection. When the moment came, it came with the undoing of all fantasies in an instant. Something bigger than a great intellectual intricate thought had unraveled a pure lie built on the weak foundation from which all errors rest and no one and nothing remains bound by them. It came running from a simple place with a warning from deep within our mind from a different place as old as or older than time. Saying without a care, I see you, and by you being there, I know you.

Moreover, before anyone could rediscover the space, this particular place that requires no road map or sign that points the way. It was already there in us and giving great effort to the resistance of childhood dreams for the things of childhood dreams are made of children's toys that can never last because they are not real. They are ever changing shifts, shadings, variations, differences that stand in the way of reaching the real world. Being in the contemporaneousness fights the insalubrious hidden mental pathology navigating us into this preoccupation of never-ending thoughts about desires that are unobtainable because this condition of being preoccupied resides in some nostalgic past or ultimate fantasy that are not real places. It opposes the tendencies to replace the little bit of ourselves that we have in all of us.

I finally found a quite space to hit the books. Now if I could only get through these twelve algebraic practice problems I should be able to ace this afternoon's exam, but I am finding the twelve labors of Hercules to be easier assignments.

Look for words that describe equal quantities, Come on brain.

"Is" means, equals, and "decreased by," means it is a minus sign. Opposite, always means it is negative.

Equation,

N - 18 = -5N Multiplied out.

5N + 18 5N + 18 Add (5N + 18) to

------------------ both sides.

6N = 18

N = 3 Divide both sides

by 6 to isolate N.

That must be it!

Solve for y: 6y - x + z = 4

Solution:

Begin isolating y by adding x and subtracting z from both sides.

6y - x + z = 4 Original equation.

+ x - z = 4 + x - z Add (x - z) to both sides.

6y = 4 + x - z

Divide each term by 6

6y 4 x z

---

6 6 6 6

2 x z

y = - + - - -

3 6 6

I still have variables in the answer. Look at notes, where are my notes, here.

When you have more than one equation with the same variables, you can use this process to solve for all the variables and get a constant for an answer. When you have two or more equations that call for the same solution, you have a system of equations… where's the rest, forget it, next problem.

The Sun They Called the Moon`

If I consider everything, I won't be able to do anything.

This room is stuffy I thought to myself flipping the pages of my math textbook and then through the pages of my notes. I loosened my tie and thought that I may have abandoned the classic outline method a little too soon in favor of my note taking the method that I can only describe as the gigantic "Posted Note Method."

"Per" means "divided by"

as "I drove 90 miles on three gallons of gas, so I got 30 miles per gallon."

(Also 30 miles/gallon)

"a" sometimes means "divided by"

as in "When I filled up, I paid $10.50 for three gallons of gasoline,

so the gas was 3.50 a gallon, or $3.50/gallon

"less than."

Ok, now next problem, a 555-mile, 5-hour plane trip was flown at two speeds. For the first part of the trip, the average speed was 105 mph. Then the tailwind picked up, and the remainder of the trip was flown at an average speed of 115 mph. For how long did the plane fly at each speed?"

(Who talks like this? When is this subject coming up at the next dinner party that's the answer I'd like to know, Sister smarty pants know-it-all!).

Ok, focus, focus, think "Earth Vs. Flying Saucers" and there is one good flying saucer that can save the earth if only I could answer this riddle. Look at notes, notes common, here it is, "Set up a grid," ok.

	d	r	t
first part	d	105	t
second part	555 – d	115	5 – t
Total	555	---	5

Using "d = rt", the first row gives me d = 105t and the second row gives me:

$555 - d = 115(5 - t)$.

Since the two distances add up to 555, I'll add the two distance expressions, and set their sum equal to the given total:

$555 = 105t + 115(5 - t)$.

Then I'll solve:

$555 = 105t + 575 - 115t$

$555 = 575 - 10t$

$-20 = -10t$

$2 = t$

According to my grid, "t" stands for the time spent on the first part of the trip, so my answer is "The plane flew for two hours at 105 mph and three hours at 115 mph," and world saved, on a role, next, problem.

However long the sound took to travel through the air, it only took a mere six seconds less to pass through the steel. : (Since the speed through the steel is faster, then that travel time has to be shorter.) I multiply the rate by the time to get the values for the distance column.

(Once again, I didn't need the "total" row. I hope I'm right)

Since the distances are the same, I set the distance expressions equal to get:

$1100t = 16{,}500(t - 6)$.

Solve for the time "t" and then back-solve for the distance "d" by plugging "t" into either expression for the distanced.

Are there an infinite number of prime numbers?

Yes. Here is one proof.

Assume there are a finite number of primes.

Multiply them all together and add 1.

This new number is not divisible by any of the original primes so it must be a new prime.

(Divisible by at least one new prime) = Q.E.D.

Right after that last entry, there was a silence-shattering ka-boom. The door into Room B-73 opened with unnecessary force, slamming against the wall given me no warning to brace my senses against the startling loud noise and physical force that was released made me jump up and freeze. My brain was trying in a Nano second to sort out all the billions of confused synapses of sensible advice. Trying to focus like a laser on what I saw revolving. I swear I saw something turn over in mid-air, tossing, rushing headlong like a revolving ball or like a barrel cage filled with performing acrobats finally collapsing and falling apart in a heap in front of me. Apparently, that door must have hit me in the head from across the room and sent me down the secret wishing-well where I am now seeing incredible visual sensations. A brazen blur of attractive body proportions of gratifying female features had hurtled passed my desk like some voluptuous ball. I had asked myself, is this real?

Before my brain fully believed what my eyes were seeing, my ears heard the sound of Penny's incredibly sweet voice saying, "No, no Sister Christine!"

There on the floor were Cassie, Hoshimi, Penny, and Janie with all their cheeks flushed red. Mother Superior followed in with arms severely crossed looking down like God must have looked casting out the Prince of Darkness. Sister Christine was on top of Cassie, Penny, and Janie with Hoshimi doing a back crawl and standing up quickly. Hoshimi reached her hand under her sky blue colored skirt and began quickly unbuttoning all the buttons she sewed into it and went around the hemline to unfold the suitable length of the St. Gregory's Catholic Academy hemline. Moreover, not so much with emotion as with blazing speed, her other hand rolled down and removed her above the knee socks while Sister Christine, Cassie, Penny, and Janie continued in a mud-wrestling match with no mud.

"Pull down those skirts," ordered Sister Christine as she tried to tug down each of their skirts in one leap. "Pull...down...those...skirts...I told...you." Give her what you will; I would never have guessed that despite her rotund size; she could move around so fast. She managed to keep the three of them pinned down with just one hand and her body weight while tugging away at them with the other hand. The shredding, ripping, and tearing of fabric sounded like the ripping, tearing, and scraping of sand paper across a stubborn surface as patches of cloth plucked off them with Mother Superior's motioning approval.

"No, no Sister Christine," Penny begged in an incredibly sweet and polite voice as her skirt was dangling in straight flat shreds off her waistline. I never saw so many perfectly proportionate curvatures on a female's body in my life. Cassie, Penny, and Janie softness's did not hold back any undesirable portions. Possessing three straight angular angel faces, flushed with active hormones and sharp cut honey-textured hair.

They pushed back on Sister Christine's shoulder. Cassie, Penny, and Janie looked up at me with eyes that grew wider upon discovering I was somehow the reciprocal point of their surprising stare, which in turn caused me to fumble the pencil out of my mouth, desperately trying to catch it so it would not drop and make "me" look silly. I did not know what to do. I did not know what to pretend not to do. I had fallen into the most cherished of aspirations inherent in all male adolescents. I had stumbled into the eye-candy store with a bunch of all you can see free samplings.

Ruby red ribbons flew through the room like kite tails on a windy day. Everywhere vibrant blue patches of clothes were flying off Cassie, Penny, and Janie and revealing panoramas of some of nature's best work.

Cassie wore a bright red t-shirt with her trademark red dot in a black circle. Janie wore a yellow t-shirt with black lettering, and Penny wore a green one. What was more incredible, to get them to take off these t-shirts that were not St. Gregory's Catholic Academy suitable blue. The white part of a garment that attaches at the armhole provides a cloth covering for the arm connecting to the power blue sailor collar. Gradually, everything started to come apart in shreds as it was pulled going over and off their heads. All that remained on their backs were the undergarments with fantastically tautly round breasts bursting out of their tops.

The now open white blouses with the deep powder blue sailor-style collar that once went down to a flat abdomen in a V-shape above the lower abdomen were now upside down pointed in a twist at their heads and pointing to their mussed up hair. Shards of blue hung off their waste, their shapely legs rubbing against each other like elongated soft naturally occurring silicone polymers, yielding accommodatingly to their white panties.

Keep both feet on the ground I thought. Master the environment I said to myself. Your body just wants to take control. Keep it in line and cover yourself. Am I dreaming, did I just see that or did they just show me that? Wow. Cassie, Penny, and Janie wore scantier white panties exclusively. Easily owning the smoothness and tautness of a tightly made bed filled out to the brim, firm quality halved symmetrical orbs, slowly bobbing in pairs one after another, up and down like being adrift on the open sea.

No, no Sister Christine," Penny repeated, continuing to implore Sister Christine in an incredibly sweet and polite voice. Those are amazing, my mind screamed, how responsive to atmospheres. How compliant and receptive were her breasts in the slingshot she had on for a bra? Penny was so worried about it falling off. I began to lose focus. How pliable and flexible in the open and free air. How receptive, persuadable, and obedient her cleavage. I'm falling head over heels, and I'm trapped. I can't get away. Our wide eyes openly met as a rush of hormones bathe in our faces, setting us free in shades of pink to accommodate the mutually beneficial partnership based on our exchange of glances as tender tantalizing feelings flowing a torrent between us. Necessary may I add for the practice and prerequisite of any healthy society when all at once one seems to live with and within the other in all things.

Cassie swung her body to one side, slid her legs slowly against one another. Then she saw Penny and I radiating to each other. In an awkward turn, Cassie continued to lift her head up slowly. She pushed, unveiling her two breasts like Christmas presents pressing tightly against each other that were about to pop out of their wrappings. Cassie is so hot she should be illegal, I thought.

Greg Tarantino, Mike Redwood, Bill, Leo, and Dave slid passed the door of Detention Room B-73. I turn to the scuffling screeching sound of their shoes sliding passed the door. They snapped back to the door with an abrupt sounding skid of their shoes, behind Mother Superior, standing in the doorway peeking around her not believing their own eyes. Their lives forever somewhere in the chronicles of the male adolescents there is a word that only they know and others may remember, nonetheless, it remains the one word, which can account for the look on Greg Tarantino, Mike Redwood, Bill, Leo, and Dave's faces.

"Melodious," said Mike Redwood, gazing reverently at nature's handiwork.

"Ridiculously awesome," said Greg Tarantino in what must be to this day the biggest understatement in the history of male adolescents on any of the seven continents as

Cassie, Penny, and Janie were all horizontal, squirming to hold together what remained left of their clothes.

"Close the door, perves!" shouted Cassie and Janie together, but to me, it sounded more like a chorus of a choir. Mother Superior, finally noticing the boys peeking behind her, with resoluteness, with "God on her side" snapped her four fingers on the edge of the door, and slamming the door shut in their wide-open fish mouthed faces. Never averting her eyes from Sister Christine, Janie, Cassie, and Penny, engendering self-control and an ordered way of life, Mother Superior then locked Detention Room B-73 with me still in it.

A miracle from God, I thought at the time.

Sister Christine continued to act on the assumption that the girls sewing skills were equal and they somehow did this last night together. Janie, Cassie, and Penny were not as accomplished as Hoshimi was in the art of sewing, did not have access to Hoshimi's Singer Sewing Machine, and did not use the button method to fold up the hems. They used scissors to cut a non-gabardine like cloth out and blind stitched to redo their shorter hemline instead of tucking the excess fabric with buttons. Since there was no tucking of hidden skirt hem, there was no cloth to be got or retrieved in the hems of the three girl's skirts no matter how hard Sister Christine tried. She was never going to find it. The stitching further weakened what already was a fragile cloth, to begin with, and with all the insistent pulling and tearing at the weak fabric directly led to more stretching that easily kept tearing their skirts.

"Sister Carolyn, Sister Carolyn," Greg Tarantino, Mike Redwood, Bill, Leo, and Dave were trying to say all at once, after they ran through the Cafeteria doors towards Sister Carolyn, standing with Richard.

"Wait, ok, wait, one at a time," Richard responded, cutting them off.

"They gave Detention to Cassie, Hoshimi, Penny, Janie, and Will," said Greg Tarantino, pausing while panting for air.

"They're all being punished," said Bill.

"So, all the girls are getting their clothes pulled off," added Mike Redwood.

"And they're forcing Will to watch!" said Leo.

"It's not fair," said Greg Tarantino. "We all came in late and deserved detention too."

"Oh no, where is Sister Christine?" asked Sister Carolyn, with a look of alarm on her face.

"And Mother Superior?" asked Richard, incline to believe, but without sufficient evidence. Richard looked back at Sister Carolyn.

"That's what we're trying to tell you, they're all in Detention Room B-73," said Leo.

"I don't believe it," said Richard, walking to the doors and firmly pushing them open to the empty hallway with Sister Carolyn in uncommunicative and fuming pursuit. Greg Tarantino, Mike Redwood, Bill, Leo, and Dave followed off after them.

Sister Carolyn reached to turn the doorknob of Detention Room B-73, but it would not turn. "Sister Christine, Sister Christine, Sister" I heard her from behind the locked door. A pounding on the door began. "Open the door; open the door," said Sister Carolyn.

Mother Superior who was not a person to be questioned or challenged in any way opened the door, stood before Sister Carolyn and Richard with folded arms, and with a stone face, and declared, "This does not have anything to do with you, Sister Carolyn."

Greg Tarantino, Mike Redwood, Bill, Leo, and Dave angled their heads for a better line of sight. Sister Christine stopped wrestling with Cassie, Penny, and Janie got up from the floor and started to brush off her black habit. Cassie,

Hoshimi, Penny, and Janie notice the boys pushing each other out of the way for a better view. The room had turned into a sauna.

When cold air rushed through the door from the hall, its touch was welcoming, cooling the drops of sweat on our eyes and then cooling our faces. The girls covered their tops with their arms and pulled over what was left of their clothes in offended indignity. The sight of their male classmates only added insult to injury. Cassie, Penny, Janie discombobulated, flipped Greg Tarantino, Mike Redwood, Bill, Leo, and Dave, a tight lip with an angry snarl. Hoshimi, fully clothed in crumbled cloth and mussed up hair, sat uninterested at one of the desk quietly returning to the pages of the book she had been reading.

"Boys go to your Gym lockers and get ready for Gym," Richard said, instantly ordering them away and from the sudden silence in the room, away from what was likely to be a face-off between Mother Superior and Richard and Sister Carolyn.

"Richard, why don't you walk them down," said Sister Carolyn. She and Richard noticed the girls were becoming more and more self-conscious and it did not help that their male teacher was standing in the room.

"Let's go, guys," said Richard as he walked out of the room, "Come on, this is going to be straightened out." He walked passed them, and they all followed.

"Will, who gave you Detention, and why?" asked Sister Carolyn, then looking at Sister Christine and then back at Mother Superior and not making eye contact with the girls or me. The situation still had my head whirling around. "Will, outside," ordered Sister Carolyn, looking for an immediate response from me. It was then that Sister Christine regained her wits about her and noticed me sitting there at the desk. She gave me this look as if the whole thing were my fault. Sister Christine doubled down on her lower lip and nodded her head at me; confirming disapproval as if I were some wise guy or something.

"You were here the entire time and did not say a thing," Sister Christine said, more like noting an observation than a question.

I was standing there dumb stricken, why was I in the Detention Room? In all the excitement, I entirely forgot. When I got to the door, I realized I had forgotten my jacket, backpack, and turned back. I saw my notebook still asking to prove prime numbers were infinite, my proof on the study page, and the text open to the math problems. Then I remembered but didn't much care at that point.

I closed the notebook and textbook. I noticed Penny, partially nude; pleasantly following my every move and giving me an incredibly sweet and polite smile of approval that made her wide eyes disappear in her squint. I picked up my backpack. Threaded my jacket between the straps, put it on, and went to wait outside as the door of Room B-73 went slamming behind me.

As I leaned forward with my arms resting on the windowsill, I stared out to the campus grounds for a minute or two, turned, and looked up at the unassuming sign that led me into Room B-73. A few moments later Penny backed out of the room like some repentant celebrity and leaning over slightly, gently closed the door as if in contrition to shut the door slowly and gingerly in front of her.

Covering up by holding shards of her clothing together with her hands and arms, she paused politely in front of me with her eyes never looking up at me from the floor; she said in a soft voice that was barely audible, "They told me to say to you. You can go now," and Penny belatedly and timidly walked away.

A few moments later, she paused in her tracks. Walked back to me with tears in her eyes and still looking down at the floor asked, "Do you think after what just happen to me in there and because of what you saw that a nice boy like you would still want to marry a girl like me, I mean after everything that happened?"

What a weird question, I thought. "Sure," I said. Penny then rested her confidence in my answer, stopped sobbing, and with eyes still cast downward and her arms still wrapped around her; she turned to walk away, down the hall.

Chapter 11

Angles of Desolation

A few days' later things began to return to normal. Much of our attention turned to fielding a complete baseball team down at the school's athletic field during gym class. The parish in which St. Gregory Academy belonged to had two, Jesuit priests, Father Vincent and Father Eddy that would be on the field. They would walk around from game to game and tended to settle any disputes regarding the rules of baseball. Father Eddy loved to be the mediator of baseball disputes because he loved the game so much and thought he could teach life lessons from it. Father Vincent was always grave and aloof while Father Eddy was always touchy feely. He and Sister Christine would always make sure everyone took their showers before returning to class.

Because of discoveries and the disclosures of criminal offenses from this period I will mention the elephant in the room concerning Jesuit priests. I will say here that some Jesuit priests have been accused and convicted of child sexual abuse and to be fair and honest, I would submit to you all the known cases I have learned so far.

Diocese of Fairbanks

In February 2008, the Diocese of Fairbanks announced plans to file for Chapter 11 bankruptcy, claiming the inability to pay 140 victims of child abuse who filed claims against the diocese for alleged sexual abuse by priests and church workers from the 1950s to the early 1980s. The Jesuits, Oregon Province, was named as a co-defendant in the case. They settled for $50 million. The Diocese, reports an operating budget of approximately $6 million, claims one of the diocese's insurance carriers failed to "participate meaningfully.

In the Portland Archdiocese, the lawsuits in the Fairbanks diocese affected the Jesuit community in the diocese of Portland, given that the Western Province of the American Jesuits is located in the State of Oregon.

Diocese of Boston, in 2002, criminal charges were brought against five Roman Catholic priests in the Boston area, One Jesuit priest James Talbot was among them. Ultimately the prosecution resulted in the conviction and sentencing of each to prison.

Cheverus High School, in 1998, nine male alumni claimed that they were party to unwanted or improper sexual advances and activity while attending the Jesuit school of Cheverus. Two former faculty members were accused. Primarily, two long time Cheverus faculty members, one the former chair of the English Department, the other, the previous head of the Track Team, have admitted they are guilty. The school confirmed the abuse and apologized to the victims. The victims also accused both the high school and the Portland Diocese of hiding the knowledge, and that they had prior knowledge of the abuse. Settlements to victims have reached a cumulative seven figures, with ongoing counseling additional. Both teachers lost their jobs at the high school in 1998.

The Sun They Called the Moon`

Abuse in Germany, in 2004 and 2005 two former pupils of the Jesuit school of Canisius-Kolleg in Berlin told the schoolmaster that two of their former teachers had sexually abused them. In December 2009 and January 2010, two other boys got hold of the headmaster and claimed the same thing about the same teachers. The schoolmaster came to a decision to write a letter to all past pupils in which he stated that he was deeply sorry for what happened. After receiving the letter, several other alumni contacted the headmaster and said that they too were abused as well.

The names of the former adults claiming to be sexually abused as children are withheld. Many of them were distinguished scientists or held political or economic positions of power. It was also noted that some of the alumni, who had been abused had decided to send their children to the Canisius-Kolleg School in Berlin. One of the teachers confessed to allegations made against him. The teachers may not be sued for what they did. It seems that in most cases, the time limit for pressing trial has passed, but the victims want them to apologize. An investigative report detailing allegations of substantial abuse was released in 2010.

Kolleg St. Blasien, in 2010, Padre Wolfgang S. admitted to several acts of sexual abuse of minors during his years as a teacher in the Jesuit College of Sankt Blasien from 1982 to 1984. Before that, he had taught in the Jesuit as mentioned earlier College in Berlin (Canisius-Kolleg) where he molested children. The order in 2010 reveals that upon discovery, his supervisors did provide him help to immigrate to South America. Other cases of sexual abuse of minors in the Jesuit order have been reported. As of February 2010, all cases have become time-barred. The investigations at this publishing may be completed

Abuse in Latin America, Rev. Stefan Dartmann disclosed that Padre Wolfgang S in Germany had been guilty of similar crimes in Jesuit schools in Chile and Spain.

Chapter 12

Song of Hope

It was a bright sunny spring weekend morning arriving in an azure sky. The kind of sky you can hear birds singing in through an open screened window. I hung around lying on the couch watching a baseball game on television as my little sister Katie was drawing pictures with her crayons. The home team with red socks was playing out of town against the team with black socks. The score was still ho-hum to mind numbing. I found myself thinking of Cassie having given my head a break from thinking about Penny when the phone suddenly rang.

"Hello," I said, after getting up to answer it.

"Will, grab your bat and meet us right away at the gazebo in the center of town," said Cassie, and then she hung up. I stood there a little caught off-guard for a minute. Cassie would often call me at home gathering a group of her classmates. Ordering us to drop whatever we happen to be doing at the time without a concern for the consequences of completely disrupting our lives. I looked over at my sister Katie looking back at me. I was still holding the phone in my hand when it rang, again.

"Hello," I answered.

"Oh, don't forget to bring money," said Cassie, and then she hung up, again and I went over to shut the television off.

"Going to town, mom," I said, walking through the kitchen. I went outside, grabbed my bike, and sped off towards town. When I arrived at the gazebo at the center of town, Cassie, Hoshimi, Penny, and Janie were all standing there along with Greg Tarantino, Mike Redwood, Bill, Leo, and Dave, waiting.

"You're late," said Cassie, with one leg out in front of her as if it were a compass needle pointing down at me. Her arms folded across her breast, "You're always late," and the rule is whoever is late gets to pay for everyone when we go to eat later at the Lord of the Fries by The Sea. "Listen up everyone, last Friday we made it to the school's baseball playoffs, and I intend to win this year's Championship, again."

Cassie tends to blurt out something to us like some call to arms every time we make it farther into to any competition or playoff. She wants to win so badly she does not care how crazy she gets. I can understand this a bit since they say Cassie has never lost and by extension, the teams she leads. So you might think if she lost once it would make her more modest. It might also mean a breakdown in her defensive shield was leaving her vulnerable to judgments and a direct hit to her high conviction and effort. That might change her. I would never want to see her change.

"We are meeting here because we need to get more hits if we're going to win this year's Baseball Championship," Cassie said, actually pounding her fist into the palm of her hand. "So we are all going down to the batting cages to better our score. Ok, who brought their bikes?" she asked, turning to me.

"We only have four bikes here," Greg Tarantino said, looking towards me with a wide grin that was affable when he wasn't busy leering at the girls like a hyena in heat.

"Will's, mine, Leo, and Dave's are all we have, and there is no way," said Mike Redwood, but before he could finish his sentence, Cassie had both hands on her hip and began.

"Janie, get up on Will's handlebars," said Cassie with a command to her voice, unfolding her arms and finger pointing at my bike. "Penny and Hoshimi with Mike and the rest will double-up," she continued, as I strengthened my grip on the handlebars of my bike for Janie to steady herself and felt Cassie slide behind me.

"And where do I sit?" I asked her in a low voice, turning my head over my shoulder.

"You don't silly," Cassie answered, smiling as if I had asked her to be frisky.

"Ok," Cassie shouted, "Let's race. The last one to the cages bats last. Ready, on your marks, get set, go!" she screamed, squeezing my side with her knees as if I was some horse and she was in the Kentucky Derby. "Come on, Will, It's all downhill, we are so winning this!"

"Wait a minute, it's kind of an overload to bike three," I said. It took me bearing down with all my weight to the pedal where I could move to get down the hill. "You said it was going to be all downhill," I said, thinking that we might glide the rest of the way by the momentum gained from rolling downhill.

"No way," Cassie said, "we are so winning this" she continued, as the others started gaining, pulling beside us and then slightly ahead. "Will, Pedal, pedal faster!" she screamed, squeezing so hard I thought she was going to squeeze out my appendix if I didn't pedal faster. I pressed down heavily on the foot pedals as we gain more momentum racing down the hill. Janie's hair began pouring back into my face, and she started screaming in exhilaration at being perched without anything in front of her, traveling at a break your neck speed. When the three of speed past, the others pull in on us but try as they could they could not keep up.

We began riding way out in front of the rest until we couldn't hear their exhausted gasps and shouts anymore, leaving Cassie screaming and Janie howling for her life into my ears "Come on, anything that's this slow should be pulled over for creating a traffic jam, pedal, pedal faster!" Cassie wrapped her arms around my ribs so tight I thought she was using them like Chinese exercise balls to improve her Chi flow. Cassie kept cheering as Janie continued making loud prolonged ear piercing cries and gleeful expressions of excitement with emotion as if Janie were strapped in the front of an amusement park ride. We flew into an empty parking lot where we got off my bike, and I collapsed on a small grass hill. Before long, Mike Redwood, Bill, Leo, and Dave arrived and joined me for air on the grass hill.

"Ok, everyone, off to the batting cages," Cassie said as if I wasn't exhausted enough and since she was the rider and not the ride, why not I thought. My sides were hurting so much from her knees and my chest from her hands taking my pecks as if they were handlebars and squeezing them.

The average batting cage is an enclosed cage for baseball players to practice the skill of batting. It is usually made of netting or a chain-link fence and rectangular. A batter stands at one end of the cage, with a pitching machine (or less often a live pitcher) at the opposing end. The pitcher or pitching machine pitches baseballs to the batter, who hits them.

The cage is used to keep balls within a certain range so that they are easy to pick up and are not lost. The cage is hypothetically useful as a learning tool to help you make it pass a baseball coming at you at different angles at variable speed. When I finally got inside, my tokens were already bought, and with this particular batting cage, you get ten pitches per token. Everyone was already standing behind the batting cage with Penny in the cage.

You can use a batting cage to convert ball speeds using reaction times. It is a wonky science but its "good enough" to go by. Take a close pitch at about 50 mph; it gives you a reaction time that is equivalent to an MLB pitch of some speed. When I am done, I was thinking of having a bit of fun and do some hitting on my own. I will end at 100mph to see how I do. I went to the cage today and why not try the fastest one they have. It would be harder to make contact with the baseball but I haven't swung at anything quicker and figured I'd put the three tokens in myself so I'll get 30 pitches. I'll put the ball in play three times, and I probably will foul off a bunch. They would be hard to hit because it was somewhat dark in there and the balls fly out of these types of machines. You can't even see the ball loading. It flies out. I asked the person working there how fast Cassie had asked him to set it.

He said 85-100 mph that is what it was clocked at. I remember watching a little league world series, they throw 45 mph and 60 feet away, of course, some pitches topped out at maybe 60mph, and that was said to be more than what the little league weight and height requirements would have you believe, but setting the ball speed at 85-100 mph?

However, the way Penny was standing, if you want to call it that with all the rattling in her knees and only 50 feet away, I wondered if she was ever going to open up her eyes long enough to see the ball coming at her.

"Come on, Penny, what are you doing?" Cassie shouted. Penny made a soft sound from a spasmodic reflex in her throat as she tried to smile and swallow at the same time. "Come on, Penny, step into it," Penny's involuntary throat muscle spasms continued to coo softly in response to each lame brain request. Penny was in every way with every inch of her body, terrified, as the solid round cannon balls whizzed pasted her at 100 mph. Penny's knees were locked together in a twist. The bat was rolling all over her shoulder. Penny began to sweat fretfully and fearfully looking like she had just run a marathon. Penny continued to grow nervously sweet with each accelerating pitch. Her nibbles started to show as beads of perspiration continued to wash over her milk like pink skin. Penny became sultry. What a face I thought as her lips began to pout to Cassie's prodding. She swung the bat, and her squirming body twisted trying to hit the ball in what seemed a good three seconds after the pitch went passed her, but about one second before the next one came shooting out, nearly hitting her.

"No, no, Penny, that's not the way to do it," Cassie said, as she entered the cage and reached around and grabbed her breasts, trying to lift her up. "Loosen up, loosen up, come on," she continued to say, as she continued grabbing her and pushing up her breasts so much I thought she was trying to teach her how to pop them out of her shirt instead of trying to teach her how to hit a fastball. Cassie leaned her arms around Penny, grabbed on to the bat with her, and continued to tug to straighten out her stance as baseballs flew by them both like cannon balls. But in the end, I did not know whether Penny was more afraid of being brain damaged from a baseball coming at her at 85-100 mph or by Cassie squeezing her in what looked like efforts to pop her female body parts through her shirt.

Next up was Hoshimi who did not seem that interested in swinging. Hoshimi stood in her baseball stance with her round rim glasses, indifferent. Hoshimi had been staring so intensely at the machine; she looked like she was studying for a math final when she suddenly started to swing at the last ten 100 mph balls, hitting each of them consecutively into the net like a pro not showing any emotional response for having done such an amazing thing.

Redwood, Bill, Leo, Janie, and Dave all had their turn at bat mostly fouling and occasionally hitting a line drive right down the middle of the net. When it became my turn to bat, I straightened my helmet. Look the monster in the eye, and swung the bat before I thought to swing.

I let the muscles in my arms and my body do all the thinking. I did better than I thought I would. I even did better than almost everyone else did, but Cassie, when it was her turn to step into the batting cage, she had a stare that might have been on the face of John Henry when he went up against the machine.

Cassie is one of life's clutch players, one of those rarities who appear to derive the benefit from a John Henry Effect. Deriving its name from the folktale the "Ballad of John Henry," The proposition of a John Henry effect was created to explain the surprising outcome of an experiment simulated by a control group of their role within a group called, Noesis.

Especially, the testing one's progressive practical tendencies in mastering an infinite number of positive possibilities that can cause the control group to behave in an unnatural way to outperform. A team's knowledge of its role in the experiment becomes a baseline comparison causing the inner group to perform differently and, often more precisely, better than what is understood as being common by eliminating the effect of any experimental manipulation from the act of observing it.

It wasn't anything of consequence to Cassie how fast or hard the machine was throwing at her. Cassie carried a passion in her heart, which was like a flare going off inside of it. Every healthy human heart has inherited a flame in that heart, and they call the flame aspiration.

Cassie wanted to hit every baseball, and that's what she wound up doing with just a little bit of inspiration falling on to the rest of us. The aspiration Cassie carried was not for hitting baseballs in a cage; rather the hope she carried inside her is the stuff that leads us out of one.

Aspiration is the flare by whose light Man is led out of the cave and into the stars. Cassie was not ambitious because ambition would have destroyed her aspiration, fanned by her greed and private desires. When passion becomes ambition, purpose becomes idolatry, ambition becomes pride, ambition becomes lust, and desire becomes the ambition by which is the sin that the angels fell.

Whatever she sets her mind on to do, she attains. Whatever she will set her mind to do in the future she will accomplish. Cassie saw things differently than most, without the dreams that are the emotional temper tantrums, in which you scream, "I want it this way," where you are always playing catch-up to the present moment of time. However, anger and fear may rule in dreams, but the delusion of satisfaction must always fade only to be substituted by another illusion of terror because dreams are attempts to blot out what is real. Dreams show you that you have the power to make the world as you would have it be, and because you want it, you see it, until you awake. Out of this nimbus of unbearable arrogance came Cassie, a complete impossibility, but like flint with a vision and both her feet planted firmly on the honest earth, there she stood, steady as she goes.

After the practice, we all walked up the hill back to town to eat at the Lord of the Fries by The Sea. After we had finished eating, Cassie passed out two types of schedules, one for the new batting order, and one for the new field positions. She spaced them both down on the table in front of us. We stood and ran our fingers across the grids of the schedules to find out where we were going to be playing. No one questioned why Cassie has to do whatever she wanted. No one cared, we were winning and in the school's baseball playoffs.

"Ok," she asked, "any questions? Good, let's try the Lord of the Fries by The Sea's Sundae with flavoring choices of fruit or chocolate sprinkles. We get 39 flavors of ice cream to choose from because Greg brought a coupon. Come on,

Penny, you have been talking about it all week."

"Only if we split it," said Penny, "We can get three fours and with the coupon the fourth one is free. We can all share the Sundaes together." After we had finished the Sundaes, everyone began leaving one by one, saying we will see each other tomorrow in school. Cassie was the last to leave, but before she did she look back, smiled over her shoulders and said, "I hope you brought your wallet, bubs."

Chapter 13

Angles of Desolation

The rest of the afternoon went smoothly. Richard was in an empty classroom sitting at his desk. Richard spent time looking over the lesson plans for the following day. He had but to close the windows and draw the shades evenly across, and he would be on his way home.

"Richard," said Mother Superior. "May I have a word with you?"

"Yes of course Mother Superior," said Richard.

"I noticed that some students in your class were late coming in from gym class," said Mother Superior.

"It was the first of intramural baseball championship games of the year," said Richard.

"That's all very well, but there will be competitive outdoor activities for the rest of the year, and you must see that they come in on time. There will be no more exceptions to the rules of the Academy for anyone by anyone," said Mother Superior.

"I see no harm," said Richard.

"Richard," said Mother Superior, cutting him off. "I hold you reasonable and therefore, fully answerable for the lack of carrying out the proper punishments in your class resulting in the recent increase in violations of dress code and other discipline problems we are currently experiencing throughout the school. If your class is being tardy without with a reprimand for their disobedience, the other classes will think they can come and go as they please. I cannot allow a lack of discipline to spread through this school like some cancer. See to it that it does not happen again. I have signed a letter against you for insubordination and sent it directly to the school's board of trustees, good day.

Bye, the way; I need not remind you that you need to make an appointment with the barber. This afternoon, Richard, I will not have you be an example of how to break dress code. I have included it in the letter of insubordinations along with the unfortunate dress histrionics that some pupils regrettably put the Academy through the other day. I explained your responsibility fully in causing the whole event," said Mother Superior.

After Mother Superior turned around and left the room, Richard realized that Mother Superior in order to shield St. Gregory's Catholic Academy, if the parents of Cassie, Hoshimi, Penny, and Janie wanted to file a lawsuit against the Academy, had made sure he would be the fall guy. Mother Superior would have the wiggle room of pivoting from being an unquestionable judge, jury, and executioner to being congenial and understanding should she find herself questioned by just offering up the public canning of the lay teacher who is not following the policies of the Academy and the Church. After establishing Richard as the instigator of the incident, it would give a bargaining chip to Mother Superior to get them to drop the suit by getting rid of the person who caused it to happen.

Further, he realized that Mother Superior had started a file in which she alone controlled that could bring down his career at any time at a time she would be able to choose. He knew no one would question the high-ranking emissary. No one could question the superior absolute authority of a Mother Superior speaking for the Church and the Academy.

Besides, in case Richard thought to go over her head and directly to the Academy 's governing board as he did with the PTA over cafeteria seating, she had blocked him with a story that totally exonerates her from any perception of being wrong. If he should ever decide to challenge her through the Academy's governing board in the future, she has already begun to poison the well for him at the board before he could even get a chance to speak there.

After Mother Superior had left, Richard locked the classroom and began to walk down the corridor where he met Sister Carolyn. "How did the rest of your day go, Richard?" asked Sister Carolyn, locking the door to her classroom.

"I had better afternoons," said Richard. "I just had a visit from Mother Superior. She wanted to put me on notice that she is watching my students to make sure they get to the class on time. But also to let me know I'm going to take the fall with the school's board and not her for what happened to Cassie, Hoshimi, Penny, and Janie the other day."

"Do not doubt or underestimate her because you think she is wrong and her methods are wrong, and that's all you need to know to defeat her," said Sister Carolyn. "She's another one around here that gives me the creeps because cruel methods work well in an intolerant world." Sister Carolyn checked the door of her room. "It sounds strange, but it's true. Once she has you in her sights with her kind of ego, you are as good as your dead career. You are going to have to understand the power she has to hurt you, but remember Mother Superior means to ruin you. We are not a public school. It is private, very private. It is another world with different rules. You got a taste of what she can do to you. There is a weird kind of Aeolian war going on and your students I think are the only ones still fighting it. Which way are you heading?"

"I can't figure it out. I thought sisters and priests were supposed to be the people with the moral compass pointing to the truth," said Richard.

"Sister Christine is alright when she is not acting as Mother Superiors' strong-arm," said Sister Carolyn. "She does what she is told and is afraid of what will happen if she doesn't. Many are afraid of that kind of power not knowing their own. Your free spirit panics them because you like to walk by and shake things up and that threatens them because you are challenging not just them, but all they know or are ever going to bother to know. A personal war fought over a tiny terrarium they claim is the whole world, so they can place principle and civility over sincerity in a world they made out of their limits."

"I can't be a threatening danger for too much longer if that's what some people feel I am. I have been warned; if Mother Superior fires me, she'll discredit me, and I can kiss my career in education goodbye," said Richard.

"People can change the outside appearances all they want, but they can't change who they are inside," said Carolyn, holding her books to her chest walking down a quiet corridor. Richard and Carolyn walked together, and as they did, Richard began to feel better. Richard wanted to help her fight her dragons and anyone else's dragons by teaching an action, system or method by which the result is to be finally free of them. He felt there still is a way. It as if Richard believed in some yet undiscovered world on which it may be done. Richard was going to have his problems with Mother Superior, but he was not going to let any one corner him. Carolyn saw in Richard the quality of new curiosity and hope. It held her attention.

"Do you know anything about the Awards dinner Friday night?" asked Richard.

"The Award dinner is the big deal the Academy puts on for parents, politicians, and politics," said Sister Carolyn. "It is what St. Gregory's Catholic

Academy runs on and keeps it going. All the faculty is invited, its mandatory even if our students don't graduate until years after they leave our classes," Carolyn said, walking down the stairs. "No one is forced to go, but everyone goes just the same. They are only four lay teachers left on the faculty. Not to would be a cardinal sin. The pressure is on everyone to fill seats. St. Gregory's Catholic Academy needs all the friends it can handle. That's the way things are around here, It's their ballpark, and we're in the game whether we like it or not," said Carolyn, as Richard held the side door from closing on her.

"It formal so I'll have to pick up my suit this afternoon from the cleaners," said Richard.

"Good, I'll save you a seat," said Richard.

As Richard waited for the passing traffic, he notices a man dressed in black. The man was lean and tall, standing in the front of the church. The man seemed to be looking at him as Richard looked back at him through the rearview mirror of his car. Richard turned the car on to the main road and headed for his apartment. It was Father Vincent.

Friday night, Richard looked good; his hair was styled into a length above his ears. His manner in the suit was without awkwardness. The pinstripes made him look thinner. He had been driving in from the east side of town. Richard noticed he was late. The pouring rain and high wind made visibility poor and driving hard. When he arrived, Sister Carolyn was waiting for Richard at the door of the entrance to the building where the ceremony was being held and ran out to his car. In the time, they have known each other; good friends are good for each another she kept telling herself.

"What took you so long?" asked Sister Carolyn.

"The rain," said Richard, responding to the sounds of the rain. "Some of' the roads are out, and it led me out of the way to get here, the climate here."

"Well, some serious people inside," said Sister Carolyn. The ballroom had many crystal chandeliers, tables set under elegant crêpes silk, and shiny silver- ware, and men serving cocktails and other drinks. Bouquets of flowers were as green and beautiful as they were bountiful, coordinated in yellows, blues, and violets. The natural fragrances replenished the hall from men with foul smelling cigars. At each table, there were members of clergy, government, and parents all having arrived from inside and outside the seaboard town. Priests and the Bishop dressed in black with their white collars.

"You're late," said Sister Christine, agitated with concern.

"Then it's a good thing they did not start without us," said Richard, looking over the huge gathering. "My apologies, I didn't realize it was so late."

"We have our politics to deal with when we get back to school," said Sister Christine, under her breath with her hand over her mouth. "Mother Superior is watching. You are seated at my table, follow me," and she took off with Richard and Carolyn following her around the sides of the ballroom. When they arrived at the table, Father Vincent and Mother Superior were both sitting at separate tables staring at them simultaneously from across the crowded ballroom.

"We were discussing the rules and the fools of the game," said Paula, one of the lay teachers.

"Oh, I see," said Sister Christine.

"Welcome aboard, Richard," said Paula. "I had a feeling they would slip and let another anorexia nervosa at this table. Oh, let me do the introductions. That's Larry Rice, he's been teaching here a while, the students hate him, but we won't tell him that, he's mean to them and screams at them most of the day. Larry has one of the graduation classes; God help them. The tall Sister with the glasses is Sister DaRosa. The little Sister that just walked in is Sister Janelle. She teaches religion and music. She has her set of problems with Larry and one big one with Mother Superior. She is like the rock of ages, a liberated soul, you could say. Sister Janelle and I are close friends. However, she got arrested at the antiwar rally and detained in Boston. She got in trouble with Mother Superior on that one. Mother Superior was going to kick her out of the country. No sense getting involved if your job is threatened too, but she lives with them all somehow, and everything is fine, Janelle is, did I hear someone needs to sit at this table, oh, one true trooper duper. Now, where are you from Richard because no one is from here?"

"Seattle by way of San Francisco," said Richard.

"Great, I love your hair," said Sister Janelle, heartedly.

"At the table seated there are Mr. and Mrs. Durbin," said Paula, leaning with the back of her hand in front of her mouth. "They're about our age. Mr. Durbin is a Vice President of a company owned by his wife's father. Mrs. Durbin is the part owner as well, but she wanted to do something else and felt it was more useful to remain a teacher after her marriage. I think daddy didn't want the both of them together on his payroll if you ask me. The truth of the matter is that she trapped him into a marriage by giving him all the advantages she could throw at him if you know what I mean. They live in a tastefully large house, alone. Mrs. Durbin could only summon her husband on such occasions as this, to save face, which was a battle, doomed from the start, all the ways you can look at her. Mrs. Durbin insists on keeping her black hair in some style that went out years ago and thank God. It stops at her neck. Her skin is always dry, and she is always rubbing moisturizer in herself with a God-awful smell. Under her beady little eyes, her dark shadows have shadows, and I do not think all that make-up around them is fooling nobody. Anyways, she is always on time, and Mother Superior likes having such a strong benefactor working down the hall from her office."

Mrs. Durbin and Sister Carolyn sat across from each other in an eerie kind of silence. Mrs. Durbin hated Carolyn with jealousy and scorn. It went beyond the point of an argument to physical intensity. The only cause Mrs. Durbin ever fought for was to maintain her ideas of how one hand must wash another in life and especially when working office politics. Mrs.

Durbin was once dismissed from public school, which is not an easy thing to do. It was for bullyragging a little boy who happened to be too fat for his age and had a problem with his eyes as well as problems at home.

Mrs. Durbin was as emblematic of what her generation became, as Richard was emblematic of what his generation was never willing to be. Durbin and Richard were part of the same generation whom fate and circumstance saw fit to bestow the easiest birth in history, born to every opportunity and advantage, born with silver spoons in their mouths and to golden opportunities, but Richard was like FM radio when it first came out before most realized it was there. He was like the music that came out of an FM radio back when people would respond to hearing something alternative, new, and different. Before the sediments of the convention to conformity settled in to rule and to dismiss it by glibly saying, I cannot understand or hear what they are saying. What is happening here? What does it mean? These same people would never rise above their noise to find out.

The Sun They Called the Moon`

Mrs. Durbin did all she could to change the seaside village into a suburban chic, feeling superior to the town's people and what she repeatedly called, "The naïveté ways of a backward coastal seaboard town." The suburban Mrs. Durbin was more emblematic of what her generation would become. A generation pulled around like a bunch of magnets, pulled apart like the solar winds in a magnetic arc.

The selling of snake oil that the prior generation before had shunned or at least met with skepticism was like a magnet pulling their generation into the carnival barker's tent and to Pinocchio's phony island.

Durbin was like a person treading in the middle of Snake Oil Lake, trying to legalize scandal before the truth got out and before someone pointed out the false gravity under her feet and the bad smell of fake honesty coming from her. Snake oil became her generation's stock and trade, pulling them into the economic backslides from the pursuit of the quick and easy buck. She became a destroyer of expressions of genuine spontaneity by limiting herself to being a hollow sounding learning device.

If information is meaningless, a teacher will not bother to analyze that data at all. Their function is to the truth and to gather and share what is true. A learning device, however, is not a teacher, but a useful tool, but if placed in the wrong hands a learning device can make more complicated the results to make it harder to recognize when results are meaningless. Out of her entire academic drill, it never occurred to her to ask the most fundamental question of how you feel. The simplest question of how do you feel would never occur to her because she was a learning device and like all devices, empty. Like a tool that selectively amplifies a sound given to it to make it louder, but never the bolder sounds of diversity that creation carries. Therein the device is hollow and does not contain a heart.

They say her students regarded her with respect, but they feared and hated her not so much because of her sardonic sarcasm, but because what came naturally to them was hateful to her and she was given power and license to destroy what came naturally to them. In a strange reality of universes, a small-minded narcissist is the highly regarded professional and is lorded over by the self-centered narcissists, as an example for teaching life lessons, but the only life experiences were the ones taught from the cold of the ice, worn proudly around her miserable soul. The excessive self-admiration society stood as judge, jury, and public executioner of the character and heart of childhood and judged them foolish and childish to be sentenced to death on the altar of the world. The loss of innocents is the acquiring lesson respected by people who themselves were mostly uneducated and carried a streak of cruelty, a streak of yellow down their backs, but who were given power through a neglected system by a generation too busy following their own call.

"Well, Richard, you're late, but that's not too surprising to me, considering your students don't have any respect for the time either or how to dress within codes of social behavior," said Viola Durbin, sarcastically with a tone of her voice squeaking like chalk on a cheap blackboard.

"Well, ignored my remarks, Well, Sister Carolyn, you finally befriended the nonconformist, the teacher without a clue and no idea of how to get anything done in the real world. How long has it been now since you and the rest of the flower kiddies fell flat on your asses from punctured we can change the world hot-air balloons?" said Viola Durbin as she was adjusting the chair.

Sister Carolyn gave her a cracked smile as Richard pulled a seat for her and Sister Christine. After that, everyone went into silent mode around the table and not a sound sprang except the ones made by striking plates, wine glasses, and the murmur of the other guest around them. Viola Durbin took the silence to mean it was a suitable time to continue talking. "If you were a proper gentleman Richard or wanted anyone to take you seriously you would have had a haircut instead of wearing your hair up like the cleaning girl. You would look so much better if you were a girl, Richard, but you're not you know so no need to enhance your feminine face angles, you weren't born a girl." It was evident to Sister Carolyn, Viola Durbin was trying to make him feel ashamed, but Sister Carolyn took control over her anger.

"You don't get the seasons in California," said Sister Christine, in a voice that sounded more like a declaration than a question as she bluntly tried to change the subject of the conversation.

"No, and I can't say I miss the endless summers. Endless summers get boring. It's hard to believe they ever could be boring, but to me the same weather gets tiresome. I can't say I miss palm trees. Endless summers get draggy. Palm trees in California sit there like old men on a sidewalk and never seem to change that much," said Richard.

"I think we're going to see a lot of snow' this year," said Sister Christine, but as Viola began again, began one of her rants, Sister Christine leaned over to Richard's ear and said. "I never got into gatherings like this. When I entered the convent, I thought it would be different. I believed I was going to be taking care of the sick, the dying, and the have-nots. Here we take care of business, I am sometimes lost, and I am far away from being complete and perfect in what I have done and what I have become. Most of the sisters live their life far from this, but no matter how many times I write a written request to transfer out of here, it comes back denied. Here, we are like relics on display and charging people a hundred dollar a plate to see us, decoration for this mausoleum crap. I feel I've become a caretaker of a mausoleum."

"I don't know, I have seen you put up a good fight," said Richard looking at her in earnest.

"But the thing is when I do, I find my mind burning out too easily, too quickly like a strike of a match and my mind never seems to come back to me the same again," said Sister Christine.

"But isn't that the point of what is supposed to happen? When a noble cause is taking up by those who make a difference in the world, those who continue to make the difference can never go back to embracing the same old mind fears of failure and has it not made all the difference," said Richard.

Chapter 14

When the Moon Rises

Richard came in with a smile every morning. He had a way of cheering us up. He would tell a joke. The joke wasn't always good, but Richard made himself funny in telling it. English and science had become our best subjects. We would look forward to going to those classes, but it was rare to feel that way about other teachers and their fields of study.

"Greg, where's your homework?" asked Richard sitting in his chair in front of our desks shaped in a "U."

"My homework?" replied Greg in a theatrical display of confession. "Oh my homework, you're not going to believe what happen to me last night."

''Try me," replied Richard.

"Well ...I couldn't do my homework because it was my sister's birthday and I had to go to dinner with my family, Oh I argued, but I had to go. I put up a fight, but it was no use," replied Greg.

"What about before you left or when you got home?" asked Richard.

"Well by the time I got home. It was too late," said Greg.

"How about the truth, tell me why you didn't do the homework, Greg," said Richard.

"I...just did," Greg replied.

"No, you didn't. Come on I'm not going to tear your head off. I want you to tell the truth and trust me. Why didn't you do it?" asked Richard.

"Because I had to do Mrs. Durbin's homework first, she makes you read aloud to the class, and you don't give out detention for homework not being done. She and Sister Rose will make you stay after school if you don't do it," said, Greg.

"Now that didn't kill you, did it?" asked Richard as he looked at Greg's head because it was bowed. Greg lifted his head and grinned. "Who else didn't do it? Come on own up to it." Slowly and reluctantly most everyone in the class began to raise their hands. "Ok, what is up with you people? I give you a good equivalent of self-respect, but I guess the feeling isn't the same or is it?"

"It's not a question of respecting you," said Cassie, angry, looking down at her open textbook, squeezing her hand into a fist. "Durbin and Sister Rose go on and on and on. They never get to the point."

"And it's not fair that we have to do so many hours of homework," said Penny.

"The homework I give shouldn't take you more than a half hour. You cover the lessons pretty well with me in class. You know the answers. You are not fair to yourselves or me. You deserve to get a good mark in your homework," said. Richard, closing his English teacher's manual and dropping it in his hand and to his side like his arm had gone limp.

"It's not your homework," said Mike Redwood.

"It's the other teachers and sisters, "said Janie.

"Yeah, they pile it on like there's no tomorrow," said Leo with his hand on his lap, in a tone of complete exasperation in the hopelessness of his situation. "They not only think we're a bunch of Einstein's, they believe that we live to do homework. It's no bowl of cherries going to this school, let me tell you," he continued with a discouraging wave of his arm and a turn sideway in his chair.

It's not easy being Leo. Leo, the lion," said Richard as the class responded with suppressed laughter. I think that out of all of us Richard had found a particular spot in his heart for him. The thing Richard celebrated in Leo was Leo's old soul. It seemed to be always puzzled, lost in a child's body.

"What, did I do? What did I do?" Leo asked, with natural, unaffected simplicity and unreserved as the class giggled." I' said something funny?" He questioned with a boyish smile while becoming awkwardly self-conscious and showing it in his big red ears.

"You don't understand," said Penny, "It's not that we don't want to do it. We can't do it all in one night."

"You should see the homework Mrs. Durbin gives us. She assigns pages she hasn't covered in class yet," said Janie.

"You ask her to go over it more than once, she gets all angry," said Donna.

"There are only a few people in the class who know what she's talking about," said Cassie.

"Yeah, and she expects us to respect her and stand for her when she walks into the room," said Ann-Marie.

"Yeah I'll stand for her alright," said Janie. "I'll stand to slap her across her swollen-headed face."

"I can't stand her," said Cassie. "I wish we had Sister Carolyn for math instead of that witch. Sister Carolyn gives homework out, but she goes over it first, and Sister Carolyn doesn't give homework every day."

"Mrs. Durbin is the worst," added Ann-Marie.

"Respect, she's an ogre," said Greg. "Why should we stand up for her and not Richard? Who is she?"

"Greg, I don't want that kind of respect from anyone," said Richard. "However, that's just me."

"Why do we have to stand for her?" asked Penny.

"Respect isn't created by someone who happens to be bigger, stronger, or more educated than you. It still has to be a street going both ways for it not to become a doubled edged sword you will regret. Respectfulness is not like a pack of chocolates. A person's mental and moral qualities are distinctive in every one of us, and they are vital to us because they create our real personality. Otherwise, they are negative things hidden in rank or title. They can also have the power to cheat ourselves out of who we are as a real person. We might start to think we are better than another person is and we may think its ok to do bad things to other people because of it. So first, look inside yourself, not just the other person, and not just the title on an office door. Real character in difficult times is found in individuals who persist in undertaking bigger causes than they undertake for themselves alone. You cannot locate this in people walking around who are consumed by the entrapments of rank or titles, but those who get high off of creating and sharing kindness."

"It's dumb," said Dave. "How are you supposed to have respect for someone when they think they are better than you and they don't have respect for you? I agree with Richard it has to be earned."

"Hey, Sister Carolyn," called out Janie, as Sister Carolyn timidly stuck her head through the door.

"Do you have a stapler I can borrow?" asked Sister Carolyn, "I can't find one in my class anywhere."

"Hey let's ask Sister Carolyn what she thinks of it?" said Greg.

"Sure, ask me what I think about anything. What?" Sister Carolyn asked.

"Do you think we should stand up for those we don't respect?" asked Greg.

"It's a school rule in the Academy rule book. I'd rather you not like you've been doing, but we all have to follow the rules," Sister Carolyn answered.

"It's dumb to respect someone that you have no respect for," replied Cassie sitting sidesaddle on her chair.

"Yeah, but sometimes you're supposed to respect people whether they have it coming or not," replied Penny.

"This is screwed up," said Mike Redwood, shaking his head. "The people that you respect the most don't mind if you stand up, but the people you don't respect get all angry if you don't. I don't get it."

"Yeah, what's going on, I'm getting all confused the more we talk about it," said Sabrina.

"Just remember I respect you as a person no better or worse than myself," said Sister Carolyn. "I have to get back to my class." and she walked through the door adjoining our two classes.

"Can you explain it more clearly," said Sabrina.

"I don't know if I can make it clearer, but I'll try," said Richard. "All roads that lead you away from what you truly are can only lead you to be confused and sad. I think you should respect what a person is by understanding that person through yourself. If in your understanding and respect of yourself, you cannot find something to admire in the other person without losing respect for yourself. Then respect what is in you in them. If he or she is deserving of your respect, you will know it without anyone having to tell you. Do not hold back your connection and wait around until a person has done something to earn it. The fact that they are like you is enough for you to respect them if you respect yourself first. But if they have done something that is disrespectable to you it is better for you not to respect them than for you to lose the respect of yourself. It is not the missing of respect makes you fearful, but is the surrender of the respect you have for yourself which keeps you always afraid. The more you recognize in others yourself, the more you can turn back the disrespect towards you of others with love. They will not harm you because you will come to realize in knowing yourself there is no reason to fear them any longer. You will see they are afraid and confused not knowing and respecting themselves. Walk away if you want to but make sure, before you leave, you are not running away from what you are afraid of in yourself.   A stroll from yourself you cannot do. I sure cannot tell you whom to respect. You are going to have to answer and figure that out for yourself, each one of you. But if you're searching for that person try not to judge them. Try a little knowledge instead of hate, because it will be you one day that is being judged."

"How can we understand those we hate? How can we understand Mother Superior, all the stuff we have to go through because of her?" asked Greg as he clinched the desk with both hands.

"You have to try," said Richard. Look at it this way; Greg. You will have the edge on them if you can respect yourself and know the reasons why. Do not let anybody get under your skin to anger you with a lie to make you hate. Beware the hate, but know the lie and the hate cannot enter. They may not know, but you will have an advantage over them when you know yourself, use it. This knowledge will protect you from the lies. Use it with everyone you hate and those that hate you. It is from mendacity that disrespect is born. Be stronger in knowing, and you will be wiser than fear," said Richard.

"How can we do this," said Gail. "It's impossible."

"Why should we bother to understand them? They should have an under-standing of us," I replied from the side of' the room.

"People do strange things when they are injured. Do you understand yourselves when you are hurt? You want teachers to act the way you want them to be, but at the same time telling me we finally have one that we can say made you not do your homework. Now you found a person you can get angry with and a new target for your hate. It is not my fault, and someone else made you do it.

Nevertheless, what about you, do you see yourselves the poor innocent victims that interact with an evil witch? Now you can proudly behave badly in self-defense in return for an imagined wrong to yourself. One lie follows another, but the truth of who you are still remains in you. The truth does not change, and no lie can reach it or ever change it. Well, the world can sometimes be a wicked place, unable to provide love or protect you when you have done nothing wrong. Unless you can prove, you are what the world made you be then no person or idea in the world can replace who you are, right? What matters is which view of yourself you choose when you find bad things in the world. What you decide to embrace, will it be what you see as treachery or your own true self? Be careful, what you choose. Whatever it is will be real to you and choosing you will deny its' opposite. What you decide will determine all you see, think is real, and hold right. When it is safe, when you have chosen correctly you will no longer be hurt," said Richard.

"I don't understand, I don't do anything when I'm hurt," said Hoshimi.

"Yes you do, what's the one thing you do?" asked Richard.

"I'll just cry a lot," said Penny.

"Exactly, but when you learn a lesson of value, you will remember the experience and not the disappointment. You cry, that is the strange and beautiful thing can we do. You can cry when your heart tells you it is in pain," said Richard. "And if you did not cry would you still have felt better or the same," Richard continued, as he looked at us. "Ok, for your homework tonight." The class moaned. "You had your break last night. I want you to do a composition."

"What? One of those, again," said Greg.

"I want you to do a composition on what you think respect means to you. I also want you to put down on the same paper why you can't do my homework," said Richard.

Chapter 15

Of the Strength to Believe

Later in the day, Father Vincent came up to Richard and said, "I've meant to talk to you. Thank you for defending the Academy's budget. They tried to cut the budget by canceling the public transportation for the school buses. You came through. They sought to outsmart us with this impromptu meeting while I was out of' town, but you handled it well. The way I would have had, I been here. You got the public on our side. I like that Richard, look, do not get me wrong. I like those who can stand up on their own. I want you to drop by and have dinner with me tomorrow night."

Richard agreed and always thought of Father Vincent as someone he could converse with on many subjects from ecclesiastics to the front-page news. In any case, why have another frozen dinner at home when Mrs. Miller, a person who has the care of Father Vincent's household has the reputation of being an exceptional cook.

Father Vincent was a Jesuit, and like most Jesuits in the USA, he wore the Roman collar and black clothing of ordinary priests; although some still wear, the black cassock. Richard was acutely aware that the Jesuit order of priests includes missionaries, educators, scientists, artists, and philosophers. Among the many recognized early Jesuits was St. Francis Xavier, a missionary to Asia. The Jesuits' contributions to the late Renaissance were substantial in their roles both as a missionary order and as the first religious order to operate colleges and universities as a principal and well-defined ministry. By the year 1556, the Jesuits were already running a network of 74 colleges on three continents. A precursor to the education of liberal arts and distinct from the servile or mechanical (i.e., involving manual labor). The Jesuit order of priests referred to the arts and sciences as being "worthy of a free man" because it related to intellectual development rather than vocational training. Academic advancement in subjects such as literature, philosophy, mathematics, and social and physical sciences were distinctive human undertakings to the Jesuit order of priests. The Jesuit plan of studies incorporated the Classical teachings of Renaissance humanism into the Scholastic structure of Catholic thought.

In addition to teaching faith, the Ratio Studiorum (Lat., 'the method of the studies') the Jesuit order of priests emphasized the study of the original Latin and Greek of classical literature, poetry, and philosophy as well as research in non-European languages. Furthermore, Jesuit schools encouraged the study of vernacular literature and rhetoric and thereby became important centers for the training of lawyers and public officials.

Casuistry is reasoning used to resolve moral problems by applying logical rules to particular instances, and by extracting or extending general rules from specific examples. The anatomy of thinking in classical casuistry is the rhetorical arguments. The term is also commonly called for as an uncomplimentary instrument to criticize the emotionally talented, but unsound reasoning, alleging inherent inconsistencies or outright false misapplication of the facts to instances, especially about moral questions.

The casuist might conclude that a person is wrong to lie in admissible testimony under oath, but might argue that lying is the best moral choice if the lie saves a life. Jesuits are famous in applying this intellectual hammer of casuistry to obtain justifications for what otherwise would be cast into a calcified philosophical system made up of the absolute unjustifiable unforgivable sin, archetype sin, or original sin.

The argument against casuistry can be well founded against the abuses of casuistry, but not casuistry itself. Correctly used, casuistry is a powerful reasoning tool in dissolving the contradictory dogmas of moral absolutism and common secular moral relativism: Moreover, the ethical philosophies of Utilitarianism and Pragmatism are common in greatly employing casuistic reasoning.

Within the Catholic Church, there has existed a sometimes tense relationship between Jesuits and the Vatican due to the questioning of official Church teaching and papal directives, such as those on abortion, birth control, women deacons, homosexuality, and liberation theology.

There has always been a resistance to casuistry by the keepers of the ministries of happy thoughts, whose foundation is more a nostalgic feeling than real thinking. This resistance to casuistry goes all the way back to Aristotle in Ancient Grease. The progress of casuistry was stop-and-go toward the middle of the 17th century not surprisingly caused by controversy.

The Jesuit schools played an important part in winning back to Catholicism some European countries, which had been predominantly Protestant, notably Poland and Lithuania. Today, Jesuit colleges and universities are located in over one hundred nations around the world. Under the idea that God can be encountered through the act of creation itself, they encouraged creating things and especially art. Because of this appreciation, for art and coupled with their spiritual practice of "finding God in all things" many early Jesuits distinguished themselves in the visual and performing arts as well as in music.

Alan Moore and David Lloyd renewed interest in Henry Garnet, a leading English Jesuit of his time mostly because of the success of their movie called, "V" for Vendetta. Garnet, one of the leading English Jesuits was hanged for the concealment of knowledge of treason and because of his knowledge of the Gunpowder Plot. The conspiracy still holds a special place for those in Great Britain on November 5 when they celebrate Guy Fawkes Day.

The Jesuit priest, Henry Garnet is also famous for being the victim of the atrocity of having his skin and face torn from his body and turned into the binding for a book. The skin of Father Henry Garnet binds the 1606 record of the offenses against him, entitled A True and Perfect Relation of the Whole Proceedings Against the Late Most Barbarous Traitors.

The Gunpowder Plot had been a planned attempt to kill King James I of England and VI of Scotland, his family, and most of the Protestant aristocracy in a single attack by blowing up the Houses of Parliament in 1605; another Jesuit, Oswald Tesimond, managed to escape arrest for involvement in the same plot. However,

Garnet regularly listened to the confessions from the conspirators, being his only crime and while not active in the plot to blow up the House of Lords and kill King James. Nonetheless, Garnet received a judgment of death by hanging due to his awareness of the conspiracy, with his body later drawn and quartered before the removal of skin for the binding of the book. One copy of the book bound with Garnet's skin is particularly grotesque, as the impression of Garnet's face is on the cover. Copy not very massive, approximately four by six inches was auctioned and sold for $11,000 in 2007.

The Jesuits were often the only force standing between Native Americans and their enslavement. Jesuits, such as Antonio Ruiz de Montoya, protected the residents from certain Spanish and Portuguese colonizers wanting to kidnap and enslave them. The Jesuit's constant interference to protect the Native Americans from slavery led to the Jesuit's Society of Jesus' first suppression. The effective defending of humanity and the dignity of the poor began to emerge as the dominant practice in their work.

Also notable are the Jesuit missionaries of Johann Grueber and Albert Dorville who reached Lhasa in Tibet in 1661. Most notable, the Jesuits were very active in transmitting Chinese knowledge and philosophy to Europe. Confucius's works were translated into European languages through Jesuit scholars stationed in China. Such works had considerable importance on European thinkers of the period, particularly among the Deists and other philosophical groups of the Enlightenment who were interested in the integration of the systems of morality with Confucius and Christianity.

However, in less than twenty years, in 1679 Pope Innocent XI publicly condemned sixty-five propositions taken from the writings of the Jesuits using casuistic reasoning and declared them propositions laxorum moralist arum (dead on arrival) and stopped anyone teaching them under penalty of excommunication.

In recent times in Latin America, the Jesuits have had significant influence in the development of liberation theology, a movement that has been highly controversial in the Catholic theological community and condemned by Pope John Paul

II shortly after he became Pope after Pope John Paul, mysteriously and without warning died.

In 1981, Pope John Paul II appointed Paolo Dezza S.J., a scholar, to head the Jesuit order as special Papal Delegate, instead of the liberal American, Father Vincent O'Keefe is never nominated by the Jesuit Society. The Pope referred to that moment as "an important phase of its history." Paolo Dezza S.J. knew of the faults that existed in the Church and purged those faults from the Jesuit Society, working for the authentic renewal of the Church. One might ask why Pope John Paul II and Paolo Dezza S.J., both scholars, found such urgency for the purging of the Jesuit Society. Could be because of a growing liberation theology?

The 20th century witnessed both aspects of growth and decline of the Jesuit order of priests. Following a trend within the wider Catholic priesthood, Jesuit numbers peaked in the 1950s and had declined steadily since. Meanwhile, the number of Jesuit institutions has grown considerably, due in large part to a late 20th-century focus on the establishment of Jesuit secondary schools in inner-city areas and an increase in lay association with the order.

Chapter 16

The Past Rises Again

Richard stood across the street watching an amber glow emanating from a lone window below the summit of the church where Father Vincent lives, away from the rectory and the convent of St. Gregory.

Cherry blossom peddles fell like pink confetti in the air, landing on Richard's hair, and landing on the front lawn of the church and reaching nearly everywhere. The blooming flowers planted around the large stairway evoked their sweet scent in the gentle spring breeze.

The gothic dimensions of the church were slender. Its vertical piers counterbalanced the dark stone support walls, transcending upward to the narrowing arches molding the shape of the spiral church steeple, and providing a convenient town landmark. Together with the steeple and cross, it gave Richard an unsteady sensation standing on the ground as he looked up. The tower and cross both appeared to be floating passed the clouds against the full moon soaked sky. The steeple could be seen from anywhere in the seaside town. Richard climbed the long stairs and entered through the unlocked cathedral door.

The glowing of candlelight filled the massive dome within the church as Richard walks inward passed the rows of fixed benches of hard reddish-brown wood. Next, to the altar, an old doddering white-haired woman kneels in relative darkness. She intercepts the rays of light with her body, casting unintelligible shadows above her as she crouches with furrowed hands. She seeks comfort, but finding none, cannot be consoled. She lights one candle extending it to the other. She is reaching into her pocket for a coin, and then she reaches out for hope and the strength given in prophecy, calling for the smallest measurable difference in exchange for the power of unconditional love.

Unheard droplets of wax wordlessly cleave then falling from the sides of the antique lamps as if weeping for lives falling contrition. She mouths the words to prayers in subdued sounding undertones. She imprints a faint prayer with a hard, unbreakable look of stubborn prayer inflection as the prayer reverberates off the gothic walls, playing tricks on ears as the sound of the imploringness off church walls always have throughout the years. Turning to look behind her with every crease of her face to the echoes of footsteps, Richard walks passed her. The woman turns again and bows her head silently.

Off to the side of the altar, up to a narrow spiral staircase to a lone room, wearing jeans and sandals, Richard climbed with his back hunched as he gripped the rails. The narrow passageway was dark, forcing each of his slow steps, cautiously until he came to a door where he hesitated and then knocked.

Father Vincent was a slender old man from the bottom of his long legs to the top of his white hair. He wore round spectacles. Father Vincent had a strong European looking face and nose. There was kind warmth to his smiled and a bright gleam in his eyes every time he did. His stature filled the threshold of the door as the light glowed from behind him. Richard stood there for a moment staring into his face. The face was both distinct and extremely penetrating. The priest's dark blue eyes were bearing a power to transfix and hold Richard to the priest's line of sight until the urge to turn away sank away like a pebble falling through an agitated surface of a pond.

"Come in please," said the priest with a slight Scandinavian accent. "Come in, I am not going to bite you for Pete sake," and he motioned with his hand.

Richard stepped into the room. It was a massive study in an old church attic and dimly lit in a soft light that engulfed the room in a yellow glow typical of the color of beekeeper's honey and in that amber hue on a wall over the priest's shoulder, a cross of jade. Shelves filled with books line the walls. Homer, the seven tragedies of Aeschylus, the seven works of Sophocles, the seventeen tragedies of Euripides, and the poems of Apollonius of Rhodes. Books written by Dante, and Shakespeare, Greek philosophers, Socrates, Plato, and Aristotle were most prominent, noticeable above the rest.

Socrates himself wrote nothing, but his process of thinking is looked at as a given in Plato's early Socratic dialogues. Aristotle is in effect, without rivals among scientists and philosophers. Volumes of Saint Thomas Aquinas and Saint Augustine were alongside Francis Bacon's Novum Organum Scientiarum. The books continued with Peter Abelard, Machiavelli, and Luther, Spinoza's Tractatus Theologico-Politicus, French philosopher, mathematician, and writer René Descartes, Hobbs, Locke, all on one wall.

On the other side, works of Georg Wilhelm Friedrich Hegel, Friedrich Nietzsche and Immanuel Kant, Feuerbach, Max Stringer, Carl Marx, Georg Simmel, Max Weber, and The Stranger by Camus, Kafka, and Kierkegaard's Mode of Existence, Fear and Trembling, The Sickness Unto Death, The Myth of Sisyphus the philosophical essay by Albert Camus. Jasper, Heidegger, and Sartre in complete volume sets.

There was a wall filled with books on the ancient wisdom of Buddhism, based upon the teachings of Siddhartha Gautama, Hinduism, written down in the Vedas on the metaphysics and philosophy of Hinduism beliefs, All is One (Brahman), Taoism Way of the Tao, Lao Tzu and Confucianism, On the Life of Confucius & the Philosophy of Confucianism. His world was within another world. A world walled by his private collection of books. Richard wondered if the priest was trying to see above it all or was it another wall to keep him walled in or to keep something walled out.

The table in the dining room was set for two at the side of the room. On the other side was a fireplace. Next, to the fireplace, a modest chair sat empty with a footrest and a pipe carefully placed on the mantel. A simple cot lay on top of the wooden floor. An old wooden writing desk by a lone window with two open books stood behind a long telescope. The telescope placed on its tripod, peered out of an open window pointing to the stars. A pedestal near the chair held a used edition of the King James Bible, which lay opened.

"You have to forgive me here, Richard. The electricity never made it this far up the stairs. Mrs. Miller just dropped off our dinner. Sit, sit down," said Father Vincent, pointing to a chair across an unassuming set table. "I don't believe you have been up here before and that's my fault. However, I heard much about you," he continued to say, sitting down after Richard. "Mrs. Miller makes a pot roast that is out of this world, so please, begin eating."

"I've heard you had many books up here, but I did not expect to see such a library," said Richard as he picked up his knife and fork.

"Well, not exactly what you supposed to see from a so-called mad priest who cloisters himself in a tower atop a church?" asked the priest, and then he smiled. The local library in this small town with all its budget cuts is the only thing that is still healthy for the continuously maturing old men set who I am a standing member who wants to escape the summer heat or winter cold or thumb through an old edition of National Geographic. Not to worry, they say the contents of an entire library will someday fit in your pocket, being no bigger than the size of a tiny fingernail. They say this will solve all our problems. There are libraries, and there are libraries. This collection of books happens to be mine.

You see Richard; the quality of a library will all depend on the incorruptibility of who ultimately will own them and the truth inside them. At least the lost library of Alexandra, the total of the accumulation of all knowledge on earth at that time required you to carry a book to burn it before it was lost forever. Now you can look forward to it all being lost forever in an instant, but I believe I will not live long enough to see it swept up inadvertently and lost somewhere in Mrs. Miller's dustpan."

"No-no Father," said Richard, nearly patronizing the priest. "It will be great, everyone will have access, and everyone will be able to share knowledge freely and openly."

"Oh, then perhaps I should live longer to see this miracle of sharing," replied the priest. "It would be a first," he continued, looking at Richard over a sip of his spoon.

"The knowledge?" asked Richard, rather puzzlingly.

"No…no, the sharing, the sharing of that knowledge," replied the old priest.

"Everyone will have access to the greatest thinkers, writers and all the accumulating knowledge of the world and it will be free to anyone who can read," said Richard, wide-eyed.

"That would be quite an accomplishment after ten thousand years of suffering from the lack of knowledge, don't you think?" asked the priest. Richard looked puzzled, still. The priest countered with his warm smile.

"It's about time, don't you think? We waited long enough," said Richard, thinking he had given the priest welcoming news. However, Father Vincent furled his brow knowing that like prosperity to power, truth to power may not be just around the corner.

"Oh, indeed, we only waited far too long," replied the priest, reassuringly with a dismissive cutting of the night air with his hand, sounding gruff, and resolute for the benefit of his guest.

"Let's be clear, the relationship of Johannes Gutenberg's invention of the printing press, the age of reason, and the rebirth of modern democracy cannot be ignored," said Richard. "This new technology will reawaken the ancient Greek and Roman traditions of debate by bringing the wisest course of actions through the free exchange of knowledge, opinions, and ideas. There is an essential connection between literacy and liberty and it will herald a new age of enlightenment."

"Yes, but let's not forget about the zealots and a personal favorite of mine, the religious nut jobs. I was called that you know," said the priest. "But now you have me curious, how do you deal with the fact that claims of reason have justified the most appalling of human genocides, Richard? The scientific racism and anti-Semitism, the rise of Reich, all had reasoned enough to kill and to justify intellectually in their minds the murder of the innocent," said the priest before he wiped his mouth with a napkin. "I'm not disagreeing. I find what you say about man's ability to reason worthy of note. What about the increased cynicism, distrust, and the fact, eventually, even as far back as the printing press, the efforts to manipulate public opinion and to selectively control, information grows increasingly sophisticated with each new technology gives me a reason to pause, why not you?" Richard caught himself involuntarily, pausing for a moment. "But who am I to say being a simple priest who has to run across the street to take a telephone call."

Richard looked at him twice and smiled, had he made a mistake about the priest. He wondered was the priest just a frightened old man concealed in the old world and hiding in his books. Besides, the church isn't exactly a democracy passing out helpful coping suggestions. After all, the established church even has a sordid history of working out deals with its tyrants resulting in the church gaining power in exchange for the despot's public absolution, hardly pro-democratic. Change can be forbidding. Richard thought that he might have presented the technology at too much a dizzying pace. He wondered if change made the priest afraid. Also, he thought that when fear squeezes out reason it forces people to feel a need to cling to the certainty of absolute faith. The dogma of blind faith runs in to fill the vacuum left behind in reason's absence, Richard thought. Perhaps the priest had become hard of hearing in his old age. As long as we are not using logic and reason as tools to examine the ideas of government policies and its laws he might as well be mad, Richard thought.

"The lack of information corrupts the democratic process," said Richard, loudly. "The people must act as the go-between to great wealth and great power, and that requires they be informed. Otherwise, our freedom will become a fraud."

"Oh, I agree completely with you. Richard is there something wrong?" asked the priest.

"No," said Richard, looking puzzlingly at the priest.

"Good, good, wouldn't want you to worry about the church bell suddenly going off up here above us and jolting you out of your senses. I promise you it will never ring while we are up here. I control it with a timer. It is set for Sundays. However, some people insist on sitting there worrying. They start to behave strangely in anticipation of the sound of a loud bell suddenly going off. They start to raise their voices as if expecting the bats to come out of the belfry. So to speak." said the priest.

"Really," said Richard.

"Yes," said the priest. "Some people erupt in relatively high volume. I am certain of it." After an awkward moment, the priest continued and asked, "Do you believe in good?"

"Yes," replied Richard.

"Do you believe in evil?" asked the priest.

"It depends on, things are not always black and white," said Richard.

"It is important that you understand this above all else. To the degree one believes in good is in direct proportion to one's recognition of evil. The one cannot be without the other. To the extent, a person believes in good is the extent that person will recognize its opposite by contrast," said the priest.

"But things in life are not that naive," said Richard.

"No, my boy, things are indeed simple. Otherwise, we would constantly be in a state of profound confusion made possible by our insistence that the same house can stand on two foundations. The mind is unconfused by the render of the faculty of reason. However, a separated or divided mind must be confused because it is necessarily uncertain about what it is. It has to be in a struggle because it is out of accord with itself. These specific ways the mind considers, strangers to each other, and this is the substance of the fear-prone environment, in which attack is always possible, but it is never justifiable. Do you believe that attack is a legitimate action?" the priest asked him.

"No," answered Richard. "A person who uses his fist in violence has run out of ideas, and I have not, run out of ideas."

"Good, then you believe in the concept of forgiveness," said the priest, "the unconditional forgiveness of the sins of the world."

"I don't think I would go that far," said Richard.

"Yes, of course, it must be my habit of always talking business," said the priest.

"After all you can't apply forgiveness to everyone. I would not ask forgiveness to those who would sell out citizen and country for the love of money, and you can't ask forgiveness of despots and tyrants who use their power arbitrarily and oppressively to murder their people," said Richard.

"Unfortunately, the unforgiving mind does not believe that giving and receiving are the same. So, I do not have the authority nor do I have the liberty to agree on an occupational hazard," said the priest. So, for you, forgiveness is a selective remembering based not on your selection, think~. Some people you would turn into your immortal enemies because you are not willing to forgive, correct?" The priest looked for a nod, but given none, he continued.

"The figures are but the shadows you witness, made by you to be carried by you to demonstrate to you he did what he did not do and because you bring them, you will always hear them. And you who keep them by your choice do not understand how they came into your mind, and what their purpose to you must be. They depict the evil that you think done to you. You carry them with you only that you may bring back evil for evil, wishing that their witness would enable you to think guiltily of more of the same kind and not harm yourself. The unforgiving always speak to you calling for vengeance and your relationships to them are very insane. Without exclusion, these relationships have as their purpose the rejection of the truth about the other, and you is why whatever reminds you of your past resentment is strong enough to justify your attack. Retaliation attracts you no matter the associations by which you arrive at these connections that come to you making you want to retaliate. Nevertheless, these associations have the ability and power to distort reality is why they call them shadows."

"Father, with all due respect I must disagree with you," said Richard. "With ideas like these tyrants and tin pot dictators would soon take power and throw this world into a new Dark Age that would rival the Middle Ages in viciousness towards human rights and towards science."

"You're misunderstanding me," said the priest, "look around you. I have been searching all by life. I have traveled the world and arrived in places you could never have known about in search of an answer to why God allows suffering to go on. It has led me to many people and many religions. Had I not seen? Had I not been blind? Then I may not have had considered what I am about to tell you.

Let this tired old priest say to you. All the knowledge and all the religions have led to what I am trying to say to you and must tell you. Do not take the many useless journeys that have led me nowhere as a priest but may help you as just a man to save you time because you are where I have started. I have returned to where I began."

"I don't think you will be changing my mind on this one," said Richard.

"Good, then you will humor this old priest for a little longer," said the priest as he pulled his chair out from the table and Richard followed, both being finished with the meal Mrs. Miller had prepared for them. "What if I told you that the world you are in wasn't real? The world you see was like a dream illusion of reality. God cannot create it, for what He creates must be like Him. Now stay with me. Imagine there is nothing you see that will not pass away."

"Father, I...," said Richard.

"Some things will last in time a little longer," said the priest, interrupting. "But time will come to you when all things to see will end not with your death, but rather with their end. Moreover, the eyes in your head are not the means by which you truly see. Try to imagine further those illusions of reality that they look upon only leading to more illusion. Therefore, they must. For what they see must pass away for it leads to thoughts of guilt and sin. Yet, everything the ancient religion of God and gods says is what they create is forever. Their creations are the beginning and the ending with a message to us leading far beyond their time, our time, and time itself. So consider the way we are free from sin is that sin of this world and not the reality that created us and in the actual reality cannot exist. It is only in illusions can sin exist."

"Father, you realize that there were times in the church that they would have burnt you at the stake for what you are saying," said Richard.

"My boy, do you think the "stake burners" of this world are no more? Although, according to your hopeful prognosis of where we are all heading, ignorance will soon be out of business.

I am not too sure myself, but I am old. Perhaps all we need do is to wait for better machines and smaller equipment, and all will be well," said the priest.

"But if what you say is true, who can say what is real and what's not real," said Richard. If sin or acts against humanity go unpunished, then people all over the world will succumb to impulses of which only the animals are. They will learn they can do as they please with no consequences to the sickening things they are capable of doing to one another for the sake of their personal hunger."

"Richard," said the priest. "Your response to this question is important to me, so think before you answer. It must come from the core of your belief system for it determines whether you will understand what I am saying. Are you a person who believes in the real meaning, the intention behind something as opposed to its strict verbal interpretation or do you think in the spirit?

"Yes, "spirit," said Richard.

"Good," said the priest. "Now, do you believe that we are a spirit that happens to be in a body or do you think we are physical beings who happens to have a spirit in them?" Richard smiled and paused, having not ever thought much about it or taken the time to consider it and thinking to himself that the priest had played him. If Richard were to say the latter, there would be no need to continue because what would be the point of what the priest was questioning Richard about. "Think and take your time," added the priest.

"I would have to say that we are all physical beings who happen to have a spirit inside them," said Richard, and the priest's eyes flashed.

"And did Jesus," ask the priest, "one born to see the face of Christ in all his brothers and remember God and so was the Christ, a man no longer, but one with God? The man was the illusion because he appeared as a separate being, within a body that seems to hold him from what he truly was as all delusions do. Who can be saved unless he saves in this world by seeing the illusion for the lies it hides and reveals them to a sleeping world in exchange for real sight that leads to actual knowledge is an answer with but one name, forgiveness, the true sight?

However, forgiveness is not of God. It is for God and toward God and not of God. It is an impossibility to Him that what He created could need forgiveness. You had better hold on to that seat son; forgiveness is but an illusion as well. Because of its purpose, which belongs exclusively to the Holy Spirit, it has a saving distinction, unlike all other delusions it leads you away from error and not to it. I hate to burst your bubbles, Richard, but we cannot get to knowledge from here. We have to recognize all perceptions as being the same illusion and first make the only correction that is humanly possible; we must choose correct perception over false perception is the bridge we must cross to get to knowledge."

"What you are saying is unfair," said Richard. "You are asking that we sacrifice rightful indignation and let off the hook those who not only cause the pain and suffering of innocent people but also knew they were wrong doing it.

You would see them get a free get out of jail card unjustified and wholly undeserved, and a complete denial of the truth." Richard started to wonder if the priest was another old eccentric, just another old man who is a few pints short of a quart.

"Do you think the word of God's salvation rest on a whim," cried out the old priest, rising from the table, raising his arms and bluntly slamming the palm of his hands on it. "Pardon cannot be asked of God! Pardon cannot be asked for what is true! It is of no importance. It is of no consequence. The truth is God' creation, and to pardon it is meaningless. You are trying to forgive the truth and not the delusions. Overlooking reality by pardon, and you choose to deceive your mind by making the shadow, the illusion, which you do not question but pardon, real. Because you believe sin real, you think to pardon the deception. Do you not see it is impossible to think sin real and not believe that forgiveness is the lie?" he continued, falling back into his chair dejected and frightened.

At first, Richard thought to take pity on the old priest but suddenly realized that the old priest was, in fact, taking pity on him. "An error in your thoughts about the situation becomes the justification for your lack of faith. The failure does not matter to you. You make this error but are not at all concerned that faith is something which has been done, and where you see it done. Richard, faithlessness imparted to faith can never interfere with truth. However, dishonesty used instead of truth will always destroy faith. Faithlessness is the handmaiden of illusion, and entirely faithful to its master. The goals that are of wickedness are tightly bound to illusions and are the lies, which are intimately bound to faithlessness as faith is tethered to truth. Therefore, holiness and faith go hand in hand as faith extends everywhere with it.

There is nothing too minuscule or too enormous, too frail or too powerful, which will not be gently turned to its use and purpose. The cosmos serves it gladly, as its laws serve the universe. What never was is without cause and cannot exist to interfere with truth. When reality calls on faith, faith must make room for truth. If you lack faith, you must ask that it be returned where it was misplaced, and seek not to have it restored to you in another place, yes, as if you had been granted what you think is morally right and fair but, deprived of it. , The solution to the problem is inherent in its meaning is it not? Moreover, if we move part of the problem to another place, yes, does not the meaning of the question become lost, does it not? So I ask you, Richard, is it not conceivable that all your dilemmas are resolved, but you have extracted yourself from the solution?"

"But if you are saying that all the world needs to do is quickly start forgiving everyone from everything that they ever did or that what they did is no longer relative. Well that's way out there because it cannot exist in this loop of reality in the outside world we are engaging in," said Richard.

"You are looking outside yourself in a world that seems to be doing things to you," said the priest. "That outside perception is shutting you off from answers and keeping you apart from them and them from you. The answer you seek; it is not out in that world. It is inside you, Richard. There are no barriers except in illusions and not being of the truth is not your reality, though you believe it is. What you are saying can only be possible if God were mistaken. God does not make mistakes. He does not toss dice in the creation of the universe. God would have had to create otherwise and to separate Himself from nature to make this possible. He would have to create different things and to establish a different reality, only some of which were love and forgiveness.

Love is forever like itself, changeless forever, and forever without substitute. There is nothing outside you. That is what you must eventually discover. It knows that the Kingdom of God is inside you. God created this, and He did not depart from it nor leave it separate from Himself. The Kingdom is the dwelling place of the Son of God, who left not his Father and dwells together with Him. Heaven is neither a place outside nor a condition. It is the awakening of His Son to the perfect oneness of all creation to all nature in the entire universe. It is the knowledge that there is nothing additional to or different from this one Will and nothing outside this oneness, and nothing else within it. It is both the Buddha consciousness and the mind of the Christ. It seeks to extend itself but not battle it aims to share and fill rather than to take and empty. It is the ability to forgive you by forgiving the other by remembering God. What was once an injustice, a wrong done to you is now but a cry for help to you to become one, again. Can you understand what I have said here?" asked the priest.

"Yes," said Richard.

"Reality does not change because we are not yet awake," said the priest. "Without the others, all of them, we would lose our way. Such is the reality, we are all one forever, and without others, how could we ever hope to find our way home. Your belief that your will apart from His could give and get something outside this oneness, something farthest from yourself, has cost you the awareness of the Kingdom of God and your true Identity. You have created a separate will that seems to see but cannot look that seems to hear but cannot listen, but appears to be real only because it allows into awareness only what conforms to the wishes of the perceiver. Remember, deception makes you live afraid, as you grow both tired and worried from the ponderous efforts to exert and establish deception as truth, which is all in vain being the burden of insanity that people choose to carry. They carry it not because deception is a lie, but because it has created, the world out of what is not real to hide the lie.

Therefore, they must defend their delusions that place them at the center of the universe and makes them the source of their creation. It's guilt, which keeps you separate from Oneness and is projected onto a suffering world that dies because it is attacked to hold the disengagement of the truth in the mind, and stops it from knowing its true Identity. The mind cannot strike, but it can create fantasies that direct you to behave as if those fantasies are real.

Nevertheless, because they are not real, they can never satisfy. What is, of course, delusional can never satisfy a mind created by truth to discover the things that have always been true. It cannot attack, but it insists it can, and uses what it does to shred the body to prove it can. The mind cannot attack, but it can fool itself. Moreover, this is all it does when it believes it has attacked. Have not illusions made you an "enemy"; decrepit, vulnerable, and treacherous, worthy of the hate that you empower in it? How has this served you,

Richard? Would you not welcome a remedy from illusions of anger, outrage, and retribution and forever be released from them?"

"Of course, anyone would," answered Richard.

"The truth is not cast in shadows, but people may choose to live in shadows. They live in the shadow because they do not want to see. To them and only them, the truth becomes a complex riddle. The truth from their point of view is always changing leading them deeper into confusion. It appears to them as another shadow on the edge of midnight. In the shadows, men have withered away, never knowing it is morning. You must see yourself complete. Do you want the world to change?" asked the priest.

The world must change if it is to continue," said Richard.

"The world will not change unless the people who built it change, but you have too much faith in this world as a source of strength," said the priest. This world they made and the one you would make to replace it puts too little a fence around the infinite amounts of possibilities and the fulfillment of countless ideas. It draws a square, immeasurably tiny, around a tiny segment of Paradise. Then it secedes from its unity and proclaims to you that within it is your kingdom, but God can enter not. You fear the world too much Richard and more than that; you fear God.

You have every reason to feel afraid, as you perceive yourself. The confusion between who created you and what you have made of yourself is so far-reaching that it has become impossible for you to know anything. This is why you cannot escape from fear until you realize that you did not and could not create yourself. Remember Richard; you did not create yourself. There is good, and there is the evil, but both cannot be in the same mind without confusion, and you have been confused for a long time. Can evil even know what it is trying to teach man?

Evil cannot because it is trying to teach what man is without knowing what man is. The devil is confusion in our identity. He is expert only in confusion. He does not understand anything else. If his water is not sweet to you, he will wait for you because he knows the water is tolerably cool enough for you to want to dip your aching feet. Thus, there is a sense of endless doubting as you stumble backward and forward in the dark and thinking you are alone. Fantasies create confusion in choosing the possible. They are very unreal. They are void of the self-evident truths that must stand on clear vision to be real. There has always been much confusion about what perception means because knowledge is applied to both awareness and for the interpretation of consciousness.

We cannot be aware without interpretation, for what we perceive is our interpretation is precisely why the limits we place on ourselves appears to answer questions it cannot know. Only the constant conviction of the truth of anything can endow events with stable meaning.

However, it must give one meaning to them all. If people are given different meanings, it must be that they reflect different convictions. Thus, creating the underlying confusion of how we see things and ourselves.

You create a fundamental confusion between means and end in your mind. This confusion is in the world and is what the world is based on. By your fist shaking at the world, you confirm what is you are trying to deny in the world. What appears to be inescapable conclusions becomes your truth. You make faithful and real what cannot be real by opposing it, but you are chasing shadow figures in a dream.

Confusion has made a dream of a world seem real, and while it lasts, you will continue to sleep not knowing you are its dreamer, afraid to wake from sleep while in the dream. You hear the call to awaken to be the call to be afraid because you do not see the dreamer of the dream is you, and accordingly you do not see the power to awaken is within you. The size of your confusion is relative to how much the illusion interferes with reality so make no mistake its interference is total because real vision is denied, and confusion of cause and effect becomes inevitable in the world.

The Sun They Called the Moon`

The face of the god of vengeance is always well hidden from those who sleep for only in sleep can they worship him, obey his dictates alone, and must not question them. Harsh punishment is relentlessly toward those who ask if the demands of this vain god are sensible or even sane. Where do the very insane belief and power of the god of vengeance come but from a dream? Who is this false god but the dreamer lost in sleep? Love has not confused its attributes with those of fear, but the worshippers of fear have confused fear's attributes with love.

Regrettably, confusion is hardly a discouragement to the confused.

However, the good news is that any confusion on their part is delusional, and no form of commitment to it is possible as long as the delusion lasts. Therefore, clarity by its definition will reverse the damage to the confused, clarity will look upon the darkness of ignorance through the light of reason, and there it dispels the confusion. The voice of God will teach you how to distinguish between pain and joy and will lead you out of the confusion you have made. There is no confusion in the mind of a Son of God, whose will be the will of the Father because the Father's will be His Son."

"Then are we to wait on God while reading the newspapers and watching on television the world blowing itself to kingdom come?" asked Richard.

"Yes, if it is not too much to ask of you for just a moment longer," replied the priest and then he smiled. "You must not use a medium for communication as a medium for an attack," said the priest. "Try not to believe everything you read in the funny papers. The confusion is apparent. Your defenses are set up to repel an enemy from outside yourself, but the enemy is inside you, where you are defenseless, where you created an alien thought at war with you, depriving you of your peace, splitting your mind into two factions, which seems wholly impossible to reconcile. For love now has found its "enemy." An opposite; and fear, the stranger, now needs your safeguard against the threat of what you are as you make fear the safety net and defender of your peace, to which you turn to for comfort and escape from doubts around your strength, and in hopes to rest in a delusion.

Further, love becomes conditional as it is endowed with attributes of fear. For true love would ask you lay down all defenses as they are merely foolish in the face of unconditional love."

"If this is all an external manifestation from a poorly absorb internal simulation in the mind and is in some way the only gateway to peace and freedom," said Richard. "How then can you account for free will and freedom itself? How do you assure the enabling human rights of all people? How is this not appeasement to the darker side of human conduct? How does this not become a reckless abandonment of the principle of common decency and an invitation to chaos? We fight to keep our freedom from all governments that would take it away, including our own and all for a good reason."

"Richard, why do you insist on wasting your strength in the vain attempts to understand all the conflicts of this world?" asked the priest. "The earth continues to turn for you and without your help. Faith does not require such vigilance unless it is conflicted not being faith at all. You must not throw away your strength on what is meaningless. You cannot make what is meaningless meaningful to justify its existence and deny yours. All conflicts must end in the same way because all battles are pointless. How can what be meaningless be understandable and how can you ever hope to understand until you realize the eyes you have not used yet? You do not see you are holding yourself back.

Richard, is it not within reason that if you are to teach peace, you must first believe in peace? As a teacher, how can you not see that you learn what you teach? You have believed that you are without peace for so long can you not see you had excluded yourself from your belief in it when you threw peace away from you and saw yourself without it. You made another peace, which you valued more. You did not keep peace within you. Instead, you placed it outside you in a world where seeing the truth will never be enough. You deserve to see your faith rewarded. You must remember God, and what you are you must learn to remember," said the priest.

"You have a free will to choose between sanity and insanity, but only one can be true, and so it is that only one can be real. Evil is always vigilant to threat, occurring as a thought in the mind of darkness always be watchful within yourself trying to persuade you that it is up to you to choose what is true. The decisions you make out of free will cannot change the truth for those decisions are not of you, but for you. The part of your mind into which evil was accepted is very anxious to preserve its reason, as it sees it. Evil cannot recognize its insanity. You must realize what this means if you would be awakened and restored to sanity. The insane protect their thought systems, but they do it insanely. Evil's "protection" is part of it, as evil is insanity. All its defenses are as insane as what the evil is protecting, wickedness, inequities, injustice, sin, depravity, vice, viciousness, infamy, abomination, unrighteousness, ungodliness, heinousness and all its vessels, the despot, the oppressor, and the tyrant.

However, a free will cannot live in the unsound mind for it has no attribute that is insane, being a part of reason. Free will enable the choice between illusion and reality. Any relationship of free will to delusions, which is Satan's chief defense, must, therefore, be insane. The vision of real beauty or the mask of deformity, the actual world or the world of guilt and fear, truth or delusion, freedom or slavery be ever vigilant know this. Whatever you choose you will endow with beauty and reality because the choice depends on which you value more. You can never choose except between good and evil. Thought systems are but true or false, and all their attributes come simply from what they are. Only the thoughts in the mind of God are real. Moreover, all that comes from them must arise from what they are, and is as real as is the Source from which they came."

"Then judgment must extend insanity as forgiveness must extend reality," said Richard.

"Yes," said the priest. "However the world seeks dependence on one's judgment as to the standard for maturity and strength and therein lays the confusion. Judgment is a knife that stabs against the truth. It splits off the truth as if it were a thing apart and alien. Then a personal opinion makes of it what you would have the truth be. Judgment is the sustaining device, which maintains the delusion. Judgment is a misunderstanding by the world because it substitutes judgment for wisdom and is confused with truth. A person is capable of "good" and "bad" judgment, and the intention is for strengthening the good and minimizing the bad.

It is also necessary to realize, not that you should not judge, but that you do not have the power to judge.

Therefore, in becoming more honest with yourself you will recognize that judgment is always impossible and you will eventually no longer attempt it, so judgment is set free to work through you rather than by you. In giving up judgment, you are merely giving up an illusion; or better, a delusion of giving it up. The acknowledgment that judgment in the usual sense is impossible is not a sentiment but a fact for to judge anything rightly; one would have to be wholly aware of an impossible wider range of things, past, present and to come. One would have to recognize in advance the consequences of the judgments on how it affects everyone and everything. Moreover, one would have to be certain there is no distortion in the perception that the judgment would be wholly fair to everyone on whom it rests presently and in the future. Who is in a position to do this? Who except in pretentious delusion would claim this for himself?"

"Are not men of laws?' asked Richard, "and without such a claim to the law is not the fabric of civilization unwoven, leaving no one free?"

"We are men of laws, but not the laws of men," replied the priest. "You may recall the many times we believe we know all the pieces of information we need to make our judgment, and now, remember the time we were mistaken. Is there anybody who has not had this happen to them? Do you know how numerous the times we think we are right, without ever knowing we were wrong? Let me answer this for you. They are legion.

Why would you choose to defend such an arbitrary basis for decision-making? Men do not know all the facts; past, present and to come. People do not know all the effects of their judgment on everyone and everything. Nevertheless, there is He who is wholly fair to everyone, for there is no distortion in His Wisdom for His Wisdom is not judgment; it is the relinquishment of judgment. Therefore, all judgment can be set down, not with remorse but with a sigh of thankfulness, because you are finally free from a burden once so great that you could only stumble and weaken beneath its weight not knowing it was nothing more than an illusion. Do you want this sense of emotional anticipation of some specific pain or danger to leave you? He having none has given it away, along with all judgment. He gave Himself to Him whose judgment he has chosen now to trust, instead of His own. Now He makes no mistakes because His Guide is sure. Moreover, where He came to judge, He comes to bless. Where He used to come to weep, He now comes to laugh. It is not hard Richard to relinquish judgment. However, it is a ponderousness weight to carry and keep.

All of the ugliness, pain, the loneliness, and sense of loss you judge will be the outcome of what you see inside you. Moreover, what can ever come of it but the wasting of time, the growing hopelessness; of appalling depths of despair and the fear of death; all these have come from you. Justice can only come by divine correction to injustice for injustice is the basis for all the judgments of the world. Justice corrects the misinterpretations from which injustice arises, and removes them. Neither justice nor injustice remembers from where we came for neither justice nor injustice exists behind the gates of

Eden where error is impossible and correction meaningless.

In this world, however, forgiveness depends on justice, since all attack can only be unjust. Justice belongs to the Holy Spirit's verdict upon the world. Except in His judgment, justice is unattainable, for no one in the world is capable of making only interpretations and laying all injustices aside. Justice, like its opposite, is an interpretation. His is, however, the one interpretation that leads to truth, possible because, while it is not true in itself, He being the appointed emissary of justice includes nothing that opposes truth and no conflict can exist between justice and truth."

'Then the only justice that exists is divine, and since we are divine in reality there is no justice only truth, and therefore, we must be in the simulated reality, in a transcendent universe." said Richard.

"Yes, simultaneously existing both metaphysically and physically in another dimension. A flat piece of paper lays both on its surface and on its side at the same time, but in different dimensions. We can only perceive one or the other at one time, but we can think dimensionally, proving the existence of another dimension linking them both," said the priest.

"That which relates or belongs to or about the past stems from injustice. But here the lens which is held before the body's eyes distorts the perception and brings the witness of the distorted perception back to the mind that created the lens and holds it very dear. Both exclusively and haphazardly through this lens is every idea of the world seen built up in just this way. Onto this plane, this blank sheet, is a judgment projected wholly from your sense of injustice? Give up this lens of warped perception through which it looks to and at you as sins are detected and justified by elaborate ideas of self-importance where in this space a world of forgiveness has no place, for not one "sin" is not forever.

Now judgment belongs to Him and not to you. You are afraid no more and do not see the hate and fear for you are a creation of your Creator and enemy to Him no more. Pray for God's justice, and do not confuse His mercy with your insanity. You have the image and power of God in you and can make the perception of whatever picture your mind desires to see, but there can only be knowledge of the Will of creation that is true. Remember justice points to Heaven and must be impartial to your choice if you are to be a Son of creation and creation is to be of God. He accepts all evidence of this fact brought before Him, omitting nothing, and assessing nothing as separate and apart from all the rest. From this one standpoint does He judge, and this alone as all attack and condemnation become meaningless and indefensible.

Perception rest, the mind be still," said the priest, standing, "let the light, return again to vision now restored," he continued, and Richard stood. The priest laid his hands on Richard's shoulder and then with one hand, he shook his face. The priest smiled and looked at his pocket watch and saw that it was well past midnight.

"Oh, it's time I should be heading out," said Richard. "I did not notice how much we talked and the time that passed. I could swear we were still in the very middle of the evening."

"Yes, it seems we have talked the night away," said the priest, setting aside his pipe.

"Oh, please be sure to thank Mrs. Miller for the wonderful meal for me and thank you for the challenging conversation," said Richard. He walked down the stairs, through the church, and out the front door that locked behind him. When Richard looked at his watch on the large steps of the church, he was so unmistakably impressed and lost in thoughts that he saw the watch's face, but could not take in the time it showed him.

He came out on to a soundless road under a mostly starless sky and walked, picking his way gingerly through puddles left by the night's sky from a spring rain. Richard walked back to his car. He thought, could I strike what I have become, is there God's mercy for what I have done mercy for what I have done. So completely engaged in his thoughts he did not know whether he was returning to himself or that a small opening, equivalent to the passage from night to morning had occurred, he did not notice day breaking across the morning sky or whether or not anybody was awake to know.

Chapter 17

The Time of Living in Color

On the afternoon of the school's spring baseball championship, no one could completely finish their lunch in expectation of the big and final baseball game. The fact that we were an undergrad group, not yet seniors, attempting to take the baseball championship title by playing against a senior class who saw the Academy's spring baseball championship as something they were entitled to became a problem. We were getting threats and dirty stares from this particular senior class all year. Because of our classes past championship wins, this senior class took it upon themselves to remind us throughout the year not to expect to defeat them and outperform them in the baseball championship this year. They said it might have been cute the first couple of times when we won the school's spring baseball championship from other senior classes, but now all that is over and we were going to lose to them, making them number one was their logic.

After we had finished dressing for the game, we met Cassie, Hoshimi, Penny, and Janie and started down to the baseball field. The athletic fields of St. Gregory's Catholic Academy were sculptured out of the remains of what was once a well-kept small golf course that the school had purchased. Benefactors donated the adjacent land, giving the Academy a large plateau of original quality grass that the Academy changed depending on the particular seasonal sport.

One field was better than the other areas, and the seniors had an unceasing claim to it because they were the oldest. The rest of us were the under classes. Therefore, subordinate and meriting a less than perfect playing field. Again, this was their logic.

This particular senior class felt our class, in particular, was under their skin a good deal of the time and we were. We always questioned the senior's classes logic of entitlement. The senior class found our questioning about their attitude of having a right to something no one else had, upsetting. We were upsetting the apple cart by persistently pointing out they were getting something for nothing and not sharing anything. Nevertheless, they felt it their natural right to share nothing and play on the best field.

The seniors had more than a small allotment of bullies in their class. They had more bullies than any other upper class that came before them. But it was as if most of the senior class came in one day afraid and decided if you can't stand up to bullies you might as well join them. Some seniors had more power and control in their classrooms than the teachers. Many teachers were afraid of them and their parents. Some girls in the senior class found it fun having the younger student boys in the school run errands for them and pay for their lunch while some boys in that same senior class would steal the lunch money outright by asking for a loan they never intended to pay back. Ironically, they thought losing to our class would risk their pride and status as if they could silence the witnesses, bend the truth, and change the facts with a win. They thought a golden plated award was saying they were the champions would give them public credibility and legitimacy and all their bad attitudes and behaviors would go suddenly from vice to virtue in the eyes of everyone. After all, why wouldn't they think that way, we all discern the winner; recognize the feather in the cap. When it came to doing anything in public, playing to the crowd, and showing themselves the acclaimed winners is what they lusted after the most.

I was not at the Academy last year when the class won the school's spring baseball championship and the year before. This year every one of us had new key positions on the field and was in a new batting order. Cassie had to game up by practicing us to exhaustion until everyone was accustomed to their new positions. She had me at first base and how well I would do at that position would have been anybody's guess, but I had been doing all right.

I had a feeling of panic go through me as I walked down to the field. The baseball players in the senior class were good. They had been together since kindergarten and were the best in their class on their teams. When we walked down to the field, I could see the other team standing behind two seniors who were doing all the talking. I ran out onto the field to warm up.

"Come on Cassie, we're not going to wait a year for you people," said Tom Phillips, a senior standing with his hands on his hips and putting his foot down. Phillips did not stand too much taller than Cassie did. He was a skinny kid with black curly hair and two distinct thick black eyebrows that looked like they were trying to connect through a contorted hairy bridge above his nose.

"I told you people before, we can't start the game without everyone getting here and warming up," said Cassie. After our last practice, Cassie made sure we all went with her to buy and wear the same navy blue baseball cap, so we could show we were a team and distract the other team who were easily distracted by their oppositions to everything we did.

"Our class is already here, ready to play ball. Why, should we wait?" asked Sam Brothers, with a tough guy look on his face. Brothers stood inches shorter to Cassie in height and had a military style haircut. Brothers and Phillips were the best athletes the seniors had to offer.

"Look, Brothers, we don't eat like pigs and come down here wearing half our lunch on our chins," said Cassie, trying to buy us more time as Brothers eyes shifted ever so slightly for a split second to check his chin. Cassie was as natural as an unascertainable law of physics when it came to psyching out the opposing team. She was gaining some notoriety and a reputation throughout the rest of the student body for being right most of the time and right in almost all and every situation in just about everything. Some had a certain kind of respect for her and others thought she might be a little crazy. Cassie was not a proud person who was domineering. She did not have to be. She was the smartest student female that St. Gregory's Catholic Academy had ever seen, consistently winning numerous personal, academic awards within and outside her class.

St. Gregory's Catholic Academy had a policy that did not promote gifted students above their age level but did allow any student to compete against any other regardless of class and age.

However, no student or student team at St. Gregory's Catholic Academy received permission to enter into State and regional sports and competed outside the Academy. They could only compete among themselves in sports under the school's overall educational curriculums that considered sports part of and not separate from its educational program.

The upperclassmen and particularly this class of seniors took that extra precaution when dealing with Cassie and our class. Having not won any championships and awards when we were their competitors. The rest of the Academy thought we were all crazy and would probably have preferred this specific school's policy, also used as an effective recruiting tool did not exist. The senior class hated us but never would bully or fool with us. They were happily relieved, knowing that none of us could go to their prom to be crowned king or queen of their class.

Father Eddy blew his whistle and motioned for us to get off the field and end our warm-up to start the Championship.

"Here they are now, relax, Brothers," said Cassie, belligerently aligning her light blue cap that matched her sky-blue French Terry gym shorts.

"Who is this guy? Where'd he come from?" Phillips said, pointing to me.

"He's last winter's transfer. Will, let's play," Cassie said in a rush.

"What do you mean? Look, what did he go through puberty when he was six years' old?" said Phillips.

"He's a public school transfer, what of it," said Cassie.

"So that's how you been pulling off all your wins this year," said Phillips. "He can't play."

"What?" Cassie said. The rest of the class team was now off the field and wondering about the delay.

"Of course he's playing," said Greg Tarantino with Mike Redwood behind him.

"No," said Phillips, folding his arms across his chest. "It's a clear cheat. He can't play. Our guys haven't played him before, and you changed everyone's field position as well as the batting line-up, enough." I felt my face drop as I thought I was going to be scratched from the game.

"What the hell are you talking about? He's playing you, clown," said Dave.

"I'm sick and tired of these tricks you guys pull and think you can win with!" said Brothers, pitching his glove to the ground in anger. "We wait all day for your class! Then top it all off', you start bringing in people we never played against. You're going too far this time were tired of losing!"

"You don't get it. No one is asking you, play ball," said Cassie.

"I bet on a clear day your smart enough to count all the way up to ten without using your fingers," said Greg. "You guys are really tough."

"Only tough when they pick on someone," said Janie, slicing through, pushing her way to the front of everyone.

"Only tough to look at, how would you like it if we have Will break your head?" asked Mike.

"Yeah, we'll turn him loose on you," said Greg.

"You're asking for it, you little two-inch second-rate imbecile," said, Brothers, who wasn't the brightest looking person in the room or on the field.

"You know, two inches is about the size of' where you keep your brain, that's all you have to know," said Janie. It became apparent what she was implying to everyone but him. Brothers stood there and continued to look like his IQ.

Father Eddy yelled, "Play ball!" Cassie was first up to bat, hitting the ball to the center field she doubled. Penny came up next to bat and nervously struck out despite Cassie jumping up and down, yelling from second base and swinging an imaginary bat over and over, trying to show Penny how to hit the ball. I batted clean up and fourth. Cassie screamed out I better hit the ball and when I didn't, she was so mad she had me convincing myself that I had disgraced my family.

Hoshimi finally got our first score by hitting a home run on the first pitch to her in the third inning. When she returned from rounding the bases, and after the cheers had died down, she was standing next to me and quietly studying the field. "Way to go, Hoshimi," I said. She pressed in the bridge of her thick round glasses.

"No Problem," said Hoshimi, "The first pitch had a 64% chance of being an inside ball. The bat length is 800 millimeters. The size of the ball is 70 millimeters. Based on the length of my arms 266.7 millimeters and their operation range with a ball speed of approximately 50 miles per hour I should have hit the first pitch and so I did." Somewhere in the bottom of the third inning, we began to figure out their strike zone, and soon we were putting more holes in the field than ants in areas of the African wild.

After we won, we immediately started gaining popularity over the seniors. They were losing hold of their self-made pedestal as we gain in popularity. They continued to bully the rest of the Academy's undergrads as word spread that we might be the stronger, smarter class in the Academy and that they were no more than privileged bullies were. They started provoking tensions in the hall whenever we walked alone. The near brawls began to increase with frequency.

I did not like the idea of them stealing money from the weaker classes and bullying them around. We didn't want the upper classes abusing the weaker ones, and we made it known by actively and publicly humiliating them and urging everyone that they no longer had to do what people of the highest class rank wanted them to do. Some of the seniors challenged us, but nothing came to blows and some in their class stopped being afraid and began to speak their minds against their class members. We slowly were becoming the guardians and champions of the weaker classes in more ways than we ever imagined. Mother Superior looked at us in disdain as they ran from the building.

Hoshimi taught Cassie, Penny, and Janie how to sew a zipper into the hem of their skirts to bring down their hemlines to school regulation with a quick one-motion sweep of their arm. Now, whenever Cassie, Hoshimi, Penny, and Janie passed Mother Superior in the hallway, they went into the auto zip down, and when Mother Superior walked out of sight, their hemlines went back up as fast as they came down.

I discovered that most of the teachers in the school regarded my class as the bad class of the school, filled with troublemakers. They continue to call us reckless, unprincipled, and undisciplined rule breakers despite being challenged with the facts. We were becoming winners of every academic and athletic challenge on anything and everything.

The fact we did not gloat made it worse for some teachers who were angry at having lost their bragging rights to Richard who never bragged about it himself. What Richard did do was stand up for what mattered. He did not like the idea of teachers passing the blame to his class every time their students rebelled and questioned school rules and disciplinary wrongs in the wilderness of their own classrooms, and he was not afraid to say it. The jealousy toward my class was so extreme; we had become the go-to excuse used by some teachers to Mother Superior as to why they were now having trouble with students complying with Academy rules.

Shifting the blame to Richard and our class was their way of diverting attention away from themselves and their hatred of those who choose to stand outside the limits of conformity at the risk of much stigmatization. The false rationalizations of what monkey sees a monkey does, enforces the false belief that if only

Richard and his class would only follow the rules, everyone else would too. It made us think good of ourselves every time we saw Richard call out the other teachers when they tried to put the blame entirely on him, his class, and a lack of rules. Richard said our class was not going to be anybody's scapegoat, anymore. At the end of the school year, the town invites St. Gregory's Catholic Academy to participate in their yearly Spring Festival, effectively moving the attention of the Academy from their sports program to the Drama and Culinary Arts programs. The Spring Festival is necessary to the seaside town to start the tourist season. The Academy's participation is needed for the town to use the campus site and its bucolic surrounding for the festival.

St. Gregory's Catholic Academy also brings to the town's Spring Festival their Drama and Culinary Arts programs. Adding these elements to the Festival for the Drama and Culinary Arts part of the Spring Festival by way of each class; you guessed it, competing in a dramatic arts competition and a culinary competition run out of the Academy's respective departments.

The home education department opens up their kitchens to the public during the spring Drama and Culinary Arts Spring Festival to hungry festival goers turning about three rooms of class space into a comfortable size restaurant where they can sample the results of the culinary competitions from a nicely created sit down menu. The girls of the Academy volunteer to be servers at the event.

The female students of St. Gregory's Catholic Academy spend an extraordinary amount of time designing their waitress's costumes. With Cassie, Hoshimi, Penny, and Janie designing them complete with hidden buttons or zipper for before and after St. Gregory Catholic Academy's approval and inspection. The school colors have to be part of the costume, but the design was whatever they could create. After all, how could a group of cute schoolgirls screw up the design of a waitress costume, the faculty thought.

Cassie, Hoshimi, Penny, and Janie and most of the female students put as much time into the design of their costumes as they do in putting together the menu for their classes' culinary entrees. It is a lot of work. Of course, there is that two-hour wait in line each year to get in the place due to the extraordinary class loyalty is shown by the Academy's male student body. The line on every occasion is always longer because the boys from the Academy are standing patiently in it. With neither complaint nor scorn on their faces does the intrepid male St. Gregory's Catholic Academy student stand with pervasive polite goofy grins as their fellow female classmates remain in character and walk out in costume to offer those refreshing drinks nor caramel rice sticks for the inconvenience of their waiting. All delivered with happy smiles; something adolescent boys are not use to from adolescent girls.

At our ages and grade level, entering the festival competitions was purely voluntary and for a good reason. It is an expensive proposition for younger students to enter in the festival contests. Not entirely surprising, Cassie despite the senior student classes having more money went ahead and entered us in the competitions anyway. All the same, our part in the Drama and Culinary Arts Spring Festival was going to cost money. I did bring that point up to Cassie, our class's de facto fearless leader. Cassie said not to worry she had made yet another decision for the rest of us on how we were going to make the money the class would need to fully participate in both culinary and drama competitions that she was determined to win.

Cassie's plan was to have a carwash. I was immediately skeptical of the idea that it would cover all our expenses. After all, you have to plan a car wash fundraiser carefully. When planning a car wash fundraiser, you have to be sure to pick a day and time that does not run into another popular event local or nationwide. For example, do not have a holiday car wash because many people may be out of town. Also, you do not have a car wash fundraiser on the weekend before or after the holiday weekend. You have to check to see if any local events are taking place like a local parade or a farmer's market. If you see that there is a local parade happening it is a good idea not to try to have your car wash too close to it.

The location is perhaps the most important aspect of a successful car wash. You want to pick a parking lot off the main road. When you choose a location, this should be the #1 discussion. If you pick a great space, it is also important to have people who are willing to hold up signs on the street to lure your customers in.

You have to promote and market your car wash fundraiser.

You must create excellent fliers and the more colorful, the better. Hang them on telephone poles and place them in areas that are highly traveled like supermarkets, Seven Eleven's, and the local mall and so on. Your car wash will not be a successful event unless somebody knows you are having a car wash fundraiser. Double check that your fliers tell people what the fundraiser is about so that they are more likely to help support the organization fundraising cause.

You must have shouters and be loud at your car wash fundraiser. Nothing attracts attention like lots of noise. If you want people to notice your car wash fundraiser, you need to have people be shout as loud as they can. It is always good to have cheerleaders or other people cheering at your car wash fundraiser. Drawing in people driving by that might have their car windows shut and who will likely look to see what all the uproar is coming from.

When I asked Cassie about all that at one of our impromptu classroom meetings, she just smiled at me. Cassie said that she, Hoshimi, Penny, and Janie had worked all that out at lunch and I, Greg Tarantino, Mike Redwood, Bill, Leo, and Dave should meet them at Room B-73 on Saturday one hour after detention is officially over. She said for us to bring our bikes to ride them into town and for me to bring my wallet. Everyone seemed to think that was a good plan so why contradict an apparent no brainpower moment.

That Saturday morning came quick enough. I woke up having Penny on my mind and remembered what day it was and then I thought of Cassie, wondering whether anyone was going to show up to have his or her car washed today. Luckily, it turned out to be a beautiful warm day, and I had just enough time to cut the lawn before meeting everyone at the school. I arrived a little early, parked my bike, and walked up the stairs. The school was eerily quiet, with empty halls seeming to have an eerie green glow to them and for the first time I notice the halls holding the echoes of my footsteps as I made it to Room B-73. I walked in.

"You're, late," said Cassie, then she smiled. Hoshimi put her finger on the bridge of her glasses, smiled and went back to reading her book. Then, Janie walked in. "Hey, ready to make this the most successful car wash fundraiser of all time," said Cassie, suddenly in what was both a greeting and shout out to Janie. Cassie, Hoshimi, and Janie had all brought department store shopping bags with them.

"We are so going to make this happen," said Janie. She looked at me, gave me a nod, and looked back at Cassie as if to ask what is he doing here so ahead of time? Cassie raised both palms of her hands from her side as to gesture, whatever. Then Penny walked in front of me, stopped when she saw me, smiled, and waved bashfully even though I was only a few feet in front of her.

"Ok, let's get behind the blackboard and get started," said Cassie with a playful slight of a smile.

"I didn't bring mine, did I leave it with you?" asked Penny, as if she was reaching for a high note with her voice but nervously not finding it.

"Not to worry, I got it," said Cassie and she took Penny by the hand behind the chalkboard followed by Hoshimi and Janie.

Chapter 18

The Moon Also Falls

Richard was walking with a beer that he took from his refrigerator to his couch where he wanted to lounge to watch a baseball game that was on television when the telephone rang. Richard picked up the phone and said, "Hello."

"Richard, "said Sister Carolyn, out of breath from running into the Convent from the Convent's turnaround driveway. "Get down here. Drop whatever you're doing. You have to get down here."

"Wait, calmed down for a second," said Richard, and then he put the can of beer firmly down on the natural stone granite of the kitchen countertop. "What's going on?"

"Sister Christine and I have to get into town right away," said Sister Carolyn. "Sister Christine is out there right now trying to turn the engine of the wagon, but it won't start. We have to get into town right away. Sister Christine is pitching a fit, get down here Richard," and then she hung up.

When Richard arrived at the Convent, he parked his car at the base of the driveway as not to block the nun wagon should it start. He walked up the driveway to find Sister Carolyn racing around the corner of their bus and joining Sister Christine in looking under the hood. As soon as he got near, they pop their head out from under the hood.

"Do you have jumper cables?" asked Sister Carolyn. She paused along with Sister Christine, panic-stricken.

"We have things to do," added Sister Christine, innocently, catching herself but, failing to hide her uncharacteristic apprehension.

"You're the only one left that can help us," said Sister Carolyn, "All we need is a jump, what do you think?"

I don't have jumper cables," said Richard. "I take it this is not all about a milk run." The two nuns looked at each other for a moment as if deciding in that second whether they should tell him or whether or not he should be involved.

"Oh, it's all over town by now," said Sister Carolyn.

"What's all over town?" asked Richard.

"They plastered every tree, every telephone pole, and every bulletin board they could fine," said Sister Carolyn, in begging tones to Sister Christine that sounded more grievous than painful looking like she might become unhinge if she didn't tell him.

"Ok, show him," said Sister Christine. Sister Carolyn ran to the back of the nun wagon, came back, and showed him a flyer.

"Oh no," said Richard, reading the flyer. It said, "Made in Heaven" on the top in headlines,

'Spring Festive, Behind the Fire Station,' in bold letters. Cassie, Hoshimi, Penny, and Janie were dressed in waitressing costumes.

Their white collars hung independently around their necks, the men's formalwear collars, covering the straps of their halter-tops, going across the back of their necks. The outfit had no back but, it did have two deep blue soft silk streams of fabric that were as wide as a Venetian blind shooting down their chest from the collar, exposing the round sides of each full breast. It flowed directly into their French house cleaner ruffled hot pants skirt. This left the breast center nude, exposing much of the cleave between the breasts as would be exposed by a low-cut garment and would have also exposed the belly button if not for the short white laced apron in front of it. Cassie, Hoshimi, Penny, and Janie wore light blue high heels and white nylon stockings that rose up to their upper thighs. The stockings were topped with a lace lined deep blue and white guarder belt, each with distinctive bright red feathering off the sides, carrying it like they were packing heat.

Furthermore, the flyer showed them in front of a shiny new sports car with suds all over the car and all over them. Janie was standing with a hose in one hand. The other hand was on her hip with her back to the camera looking over her shoulder. Hoshimi wore a baseball cap and bent over the car with two hands on the front fender and her long slender shaped legs extended straight, scrubbing with a sponge with most of her back to the camera, and looking over her shoulder. Cassie sat sideways on the hood, hands flat behind her and legs crossed elongated above the burnished chromium-plate grill of the sports car. Penny sat in front of the car at a 45-degree angle, posed sitting coyly on her ankles, one hand folded behind her head and another falling between her thighs. Penny had the innocent look of apparent confusion on her face as if she were still processing.

"Ok," said Sister Carolyn in a faint-hearted tone.

"I don't have cables," said Richard, nervously.

"They have the traffic backed up," said Sister Christine. "You can't get in or out of town easily. The Sheriff is directing traffic and wants to know what we want him to do because he's got to do something." Richard walked over to the nun wagon, looked under the hood, and studied the engine. Bent over the engine to reach the wagon's distributor and popped the cap. He brushed the years of battery crud off the terminals, clipped the distributor cap back on the distributor, and asked them to try turning the engine again. When the engine did not turn, he asked them to turn on the lights. When the lights did not come on, he slammed the hood shut and walked to the open door of the wagon.

"Everything is going to be fine," said Richard, walking to the open door. "All we need is my car, and it will be all right."

On the way into town, they found many flyers and quickly got rid of them. As they drove along, Sister Carolyn wondered aloud, and then asked, "Richard, have you notice anything different about this class of yours?"

Richard hesitated, and his silence was long enough that it marshaled up and pulled all the tension out of the car. In the speed of a popping balloon, they all burst out together into laughter and found it hard to stop. "No," said Sister Carolyn, trying to steady herself to get the words out in a thoughtful manner. "I'm not saying they're bad," she continued, failing to talk through a giggle, but everyone, again, including herself erupted into another fit of laughter with Sister Christine laughing the loudest, unable to catch her breath. The strength of their laughter brought about another round of intense laughing when they all notice how Sister Christine was beat red with uncontrollable howls of laughter and jiggling like a crimson pot full of Jell-O.

"No, no, I better explain," said Sister Carolyn, collecting herself into seriousness. "They are not venomous, malicious or exhibit any strong unreasoning desire toward vindictiveness. It is almost as if they are undergoing a metamorphosis into a weirdly organized sub-culture."

"An organized culture of little monsters you mean," replied Sister Christine," Unless for some reason we are no longer talking about the same collection of volcanoes and tornadoes. They are like a bunch of lost traveling time bombs meandering in stereo."

"No, they don't seem lost to me," replied Sister Carolyn, turning to the back seat of the car to face Sister Christine.

"Uh-huh," replied Sister Christine, rolling her eyes. She smirked and shook her head and then looking sternly back at Sister Carolyn, folded her arms, and razed one eyebrow, nodding her head, teasingly gesturing her friend to continue.

"I'm serious," said Sister Carolyn, rolling down her window. "They have formed strong ties with one another. All centered on the idea of their feelings for one another. A strong bond like that is unusual, and I find myself admiring it wherever I can find it. Even in people so young. Do you notice how they protect each other from harm and have begun to defend some of the bullied younger ones? They are like a little society unto themselves with a strong code of ethics. They seem to have natural leadership centered on what was once known as chivalry."

"Let me open my window, the horse just hauled another load," said Sister Christine. "Those girls in that class have no idea of what they're going to be dealing with if they continue to act this way."

"But why should they have to deal with uptight judgments of people who have a mental and emotional problem themselves over what other people are doing? What did they do that they are always wrong and why are the ones who have a problem always right," said Richard. "If people get uptight over how a person feels, thinks, or how girls dress, isn't it the other person's problem and not the girls? I mean there are cultures in the world that do not get uptight. In some South-Southeast Asian cultures, people take public baths. No one gets uptight over it. They are taking an uncomplicated bath, and if they have a laugh while there, it is only a bath. The kids have this saying, whoever smelt it dealt it. Whenever a person is constantly sniffing for the filth that in its nature is innocent and perhaps even pure, they should be the ones we really should be keeping an eye on. It seems a little backward to me. Anyway, they are young girls walking through their life and drifting through the phonies."

"I believe it must be one of nature's simple elegances that these kids who are so close to nature can be brought to a rationalization that forms a code of chivalry," said Sister Carolyn. "This class is like the Knights of the Round Table and this group of students is not unlike the knights that were in it. However, they may not call it that exactly and may be completely unaware that much of their behavior emulates an old story. It's almost like one of Jungian's ancient archetypes surfacing in courage, honor, courtesy, justice, and a readiness to help the weak with sheer bravery and developing courtesy."

"Bravery, maybe, if they had any sense," said Sister Christine. "There is a name to describe what they're doing, but bravery's not the one that pops into my mind."

"You have not been seeing what I have been looking at and finding," said Sister Carolyn. "You would not say that if you saw how many times they stare down the older bullies in the school, and yes. I am ashamed to say, we do have kids bullying the smaller ones right under our noses, but this group is fearless, and they are led by a collection of incredible girls."

"They can't be out there waving their red flags up in the air," said Sister Christine. "It's a sure fire way for them to get into trouble with the wrong crowd."

"I think Richard is right on this one," said Sister Carolyn. "I think it's going to be the wrong crowd's problem if they ever want to mess with them. It should be that way and not the other way around. Yes, they are developing at a fast rate and each one's condition of being pleasing or filling out or fulfilling their own nature, it is not ours to judge what God has created. Don't misunderstand me; we are shutting them down as of now. But haven't you noticed something a little odd and when you step back, looking into their eyes."

"It's as if they are holding you to their yardsticks instead of them holding up to ours," said Richard.

"Exactly," said Sister Carolyn. "They will have to trust us, and it won't be easy for them. They have a full-proof defense that even has the Mother Superior going in circles. Their resolved way of thinking and feeling about someone or something, and of themselves, typically is the common denominator that is reflected in their behavior, it has been going on for a while, and Mother Superior doesn't want it to spread."

"And the farmer hauls another load," said Sister Christine. "Well, we should all thank our heavenly Father that she's out of town this weekend."

"We should park here and walk the rest of the way in. The streets leading to the center of town are like a parking lot," said Richard, turning off the engine of his car.

Cassie took Penny by the hand behind the blackboard followed by Hoshimi and Janie. Before I knew what was going on, twisted felted fabrics made from wool and cotton fiber began softly pouring off them and floating down with abandon in tints of vivid colors falling to the ground exposing only their shapely legs as they stood laughing and giggling behind the chalkboard. I heard the frenzied sounds of the agitating, jostling and unfolding of paper wrappings freeing their objects packed in boxes and department store bags.

"Don't you peak," said Penny.

"No, I won't do that," I said, and Cassie, Hoshimi, Penny, and Janie's giggles went to laughter.

I wondered why they had dropped their shorts when Greg Tarantino, Mike Redwood, Bill, Leo, and Dave walked in the room. It took a second for them to forget what they were talking about and come to a drop-dead silence. They turned to me with their gaping mouths and then a wry face, grimaced as if I had one a lottery, and didn't let them in on it. Cassie, Hoshimi, Penny, and Janie were laughing so hard from behind the chalkboard that they couldn't hear that Greg Tarantino, Mike Redwood, Bill, Leo, and Dave had arrived. Moreover, Greg Tarantino, Mike Redwood, Bill, Leo, and Dave were euphoric thinking they had finally arrived. When Cassie, Hoshimi, Penny, and Janie began a tug of war to get Penny's top into her scantily clad blue and white outfit, the whole chalkboard went down, slipping to the floor.

"Oh my God, I'm so sorry," said Penny, suddenly looking wide-eyed and nervously at me. It's all my fault, I am such a klutz," she continued.

"Incredibly too sweet for words," said Bill.

"Awesome," said Greg Tarantino, sounding like he was looking at a fireworks display.

"Did you see that, it's a happy hand booby sandwich," said Leo.

"Oh my God, I'm so sorry," repeated Penny, wide-eyed and nervously locking her eyes to mine. It's all my fault; I am such a klutz."

"I'd like the split that like lumber," said. Greg Tarantino.

"Get out, perves!" shouted Cassie, Hoshimi, Penny, and Janie, simultaneously.

"How many times are we going to tell you idiotic perves, we can hear you!" said Janie.

"Get out or lose a kneecap!" said Cassie.

I got up from the desk, feeling beetle-browed on the back of my neck from a disappointed Greg Tarantino, Mike Redwood, Bill, Leo, and Dave as they followed me out the door. Once outside, Mike Redwood showed me the flyer for the car wash that Cassie, Hoshimi, Penny, and Janie told us they could do without much help.

"These flyers are all over town," said Mike, showing the flyer to me. Then he asked quickly for it back as if the flyer was a valuable heirloom that has been in possession of his family for a long time and must be passed on from one generation to the next.

Although you are supposed to plan a car wash that does not conflict with another popular local or even nationwide event or holiday weekend, we planned ours on Memorial Day weekend. Even though you want to pick a parking lot off the main road, ours was on the town's main road, behind a fire station. I thought they got one thing right; nothing attracts attention like the noise that comes about because you have a great flyer and these flyers were more colorful and better than most.

When Cassie, Hoshimi, Penny, and Janie walked out of Room B-73, the inner tactual sensation cores of both my mind and body went boom. Standing there one by one, folding their arms, fixed in absolute resolute toughness. In heels with one leg pointing towards us, demonstrating a strict and uncompromising attitude determined to protect their interests and maintaining self-confidence without intimidations from the opposition, confident and determined.

As we rode with them on our bikes into town, I noticed Cassie's hair caught the scent of the ocean's sea air in front of me as her hair freely played in the wind. I felt Penny brush herself behind me, resting her cheek on my upper shoulder. We flew in an excited sensitivity not arrived at by silver or gold. Rather, whatever our hearts told us there, we would go.

When we rode into the parking lot, the line into Main Street had already begun to take a long winding shape. Cassie and Penny quickly got off my bike and walked over to Hoshimi and Janie, pulled apart a group of car wash signs that Janie had been sitting on and began to pass them out. They walked to the main road and did a few shout outs, but they did not have to bother. As soon as they walked out with a stiff, erect, and apparently bold and free-spirited high heel gait, they began to stop traffic dead in its tracks at first sight of them.

Mike Redwood, Bill, Leo, Dave, and I ran to fill the buckets that someone had left us. We filled the buckets with car wash soap and sponges. Greg Tarantino took it upon himself to take the role of car wash traffic cop and nearly got me run over with the first car. He hadn't a clue about how to traffic control or what he was doing, but that didn't seem to bother him too much. Some of the drivers managed to get out of the Greg Tarantino endless loop-the-loop tour of the parking lot. His circular tour backed things up more, but it at least gave us some time, and like traffic controllers with planes endlessly circling above an airport, we were able to talk them down off the loop and into landing so we could wash their cars.

Everyone was in a good holiday weekend mood, and the old women seem to be as excited or confused as the old men were. All was well for about twenty-five minutes. Until Sheriff, O'Brien came in with his car with whooping siren and flashing lights. We all thought, Sheriff, O'Brien is coming in to wash his police car, although, a bit abruptly as his car flew up in the air and came crashing down over the speed bump that he was so proud to recommend to the seaboard town's mayor and town council not too long ago.

Nevertheless, we didn't think he had to make so much noise with his new police car, drawing attention with his flashing lights and rudely cutting the car wash line. We would have all recognized Sheriff O'Brien anyway without such a display of expensive equipment of course. Sheriff, O'Brien did a strange thing after his police car came crashing down with a large thud.

Sheriff, O'Brien jumped out of his car and started to move his feet up and down turning in one direction and then the other and yet another, trying to stick his head above the crowd to the main street. He continued to run across the parking lot wild-eyed, waving and popping his head nervously up and down, still looking towards the main street like a water spirit bobbing up and down on the surface of the sea. I then noticed him running over to us, still stretching his neck towards the main street as if he was looking for a quarterback to throw him a football.

"What are you kids doing?" asked Sheriff O'Brien, abruptly, brief and to the point of rudeness.

"We are washing cars, Sheriff O'Brien," I said. My hands were full of soap and ready to sponge off the soap from the car that was under me.

"What are you some kind of wise guy?" asked Sheriff O'Brien.

"No," I said, turning to Mike Redwood, Bill, Leo, and Dave, who stopped washing the car as we exchanged puzzled looks.

"Well, you can't wash cars here," said Sheriff O'Brien.

"But where are we going to wash cars?" asked Leo.

"OH, for the love of Mike," said Sheriff O'Brien. "Do you people want to be hauled in?"

"What's the problem, Sheriff?" asked a hippie from his car.

"They can't be washing cars here," repeated Sheriff O'Brien.

"Well, Sheriff, where do you think they should wash cars?" questioned the other hippie.

"I'm sure they can be here," said the other hippie from the same car. "These are students from St. Gregory Catholic Academy and from what I understand the permission was given out of your department."

"St. Gregory School, huh," said Sheriff O'Brien. "I had better call them to get someone down here before this gets any further out of hand." He turned his head quickly to see Greg Tarantino waving more cars into nowhere. "OH, for the love of Mike, kid do you want to stop that, just stop it right there."

The Sheriff return to his car got in and drove on the sidewalk, down the wrong way of the street, pass stopped cars backing up and honking their horns on all sides of him. Cassie, Hoshimi, Penny, and Janie walked over as people broke out clapping and cheering.

"How's it going out there," I said.

"Great," said Cassie. "We are going to create a fortune for the Spring Festival. We have cars backed up for miles wanting to wash their cars here. There is no need for us to be standing out there, jumping up and down like jumping beans to get people's attention. Getting the town's attention was a complete success, So, we thought you guys could use some help washing cars."

"And it's really hot," added Penny, bouncing up and down, fanning herself with her hand, beads of sweat had formed on the top of her milk lips and around the cleavage of her sultry milk sacks that seemed to be resisting the gravity of popping completely out of her top. Cassie, Hoshimi, Penny, and Janie all appeared to be "defying" the law of gravity that day. "Can we help you guys?"

"Oh, sure you can," I said, with Greg Tarantino, Mike Redwood, Bill, Leo, and Dave all nodding silently in agreement.

"How do we do this?" asked Penny.

"We will do all the washing. Just pick up the hoses and rinse the cars off when we tell you," said Leo.

As each car rinsed off, Cassie, Hoshimi, Penny, and Janie managed to find a way to get some extra water on at least one of us. At first, it was by chance then it was with a giggle, and then it came with a laugh. Soon we realized that they either wanted to get wet to cool off from the heat, or they were going to get wet for being funny, but they wanted to get wet. Then Cassie after rinsing a car bent over without so some much as bending a knee and poured water on my jeans and face while pretending to reach for the bucket of soap.

"What?" Cassie said, looking right at me with a half sort of grin. "What? Can't get wet at a car wash, big baby?" I ripped off my wet tee shirt and began to scrub the next car with her eyes still on me. Still, I wondered along with the rest when I might get her sweaty body, wet.

I finished washing the next car. Cassie remained standing taut from head to toecap, holding the top of an open hose like some future warrior princess holding a broken bow as the water continued to pour out making a broad ark to her side like she just freed an arrow that was beautiful. Cassie looked excessively hot to touch.

"Wait, wait," I said. "We're not done here."

Cassie was gently moving like the Guinevere of her court as foam like white lace, and silky velvets fell sparkling off her slender fingers with royalty and grace shooting a bittersweet look back over her shoulder to Hoshimi, Penny, and Janie as if she was going to knock me off my feet.

I scooped out two large handfuls of soapsuds and placed them on her chest. Greg, Mike, Bill, Leo, and Dave scooped up a large handful of suds as well and flicked the suds onto Hoshimi, Penny, and Janie.

Fear cannot gladden. Love does. Fear makes exclusions. Love never does. Fear invites dissociation because it brings with it the weakness of separation. Love invites harmony because it brings with it the strength of unity. Everything of love can be counted on because everything of love is real.

Love is the universal constant of the stars because it is inspired by the harmony of all living things, and is in accord with all of life's laws. Since it is love's true meaning, it is also ours. Love cannot be out of accord with itself. Our meaning could not be out of accord with love because our whole meaning and our only meaning came from love and was like love. We could not separate ourselves from love's creation, which created us by sharing love's being through us.

The Sun They Called the Moon`

Understanding means consistency because love's laws are consistent and because we understood, we identified with making love a part of us.

True learning is constant and so vital in its power for change that even a child of love can recognize his or her power in changing his or her mind in one instant and changing the world in the next.

The unknowing learner is the unloving lover of the world demanding gratitude from us but is not grateful to us. That is because he or she thinks he or she is giving something to us and is not receiving something equally desirable in return. Their lessons have a limit they create by their ingratitude, and since we teach what we know, theirs is the limiting teachings of fear. Our learning of the world's direct or indirect teachings carries with it the hidden dangers of arriving at the place where learning so much teaches so little.

The Sun They Called the Moon`

"You guys are dead," said Cassie by the car wheels, standing straight up in her blue high heels as water, suds, and laughter came exploding, spinning, swinging madly over everyone. We slid and slipped lightly in the sun. I put my arms around Cassie, taking the hose not aiming at anyone. "You jerk; you got me all wet," she continued, not trying to escape to go and run, wittingly poking her legs and feet and taking a dare to trip me, accompanied by the sun, far beneath the weight of every single hate, not aimed at anyone.

"Hey, I'll save you," said Penny, drinking in all the sun around her. Then she took aim with her hose and shot a steady torrent of water at our heads and faces, standing there under a clear blue sky that had no limits as if she were playing of all places on a windy beach far from the tangled reach of the old-familiar positions of right and wrong. Far outside the foggy ruins of walking zombies and the mind left broken. Far from the fools who sleep. Far from the broken polished, slick Ravens that creep but not unlike being safe inside the circle of time like the returning tumbling sand that runs through it in a moment left unspoken knowing the refusal to acknowledge love is fear's only invitation and must not be woken.

"Get her back, no, I'll soak the pretty witch, myself," said Cassie, laughing in a headlong descent for the hose, pushing her bottom into my shorts. By chance, I crossed my arm to her hand, pulled, and spun her; the other arm suddenly sent unwinding out after her, waving free, slipping momentarily beneath the transparent sky where breathing unexpectedly began to feel like something new.

Then I heard the unfocused tracings of skipping' twists in uneven rhyme of uncomprehending verse, off of the smiles of all the people speaking in a single language, all speaking with the same smile without a single curse. Disappearing' into the hollow rings of time, escaping and on the run and paying any mind to the unloving lovers of the world. Cheering at the defeated and done liars left behind, staggering across the road, silhouetted by the sea, and driven deep beneath the waves like seaweed kings brought down by the weight of their golden rings as not much else at the end of the day can pass away.

A shrill sound of a whistle started hammering into the air, repeatedly, steadily, and dementedly like a kettle that gives a scream when steam escapes through it, indicating that the water in it is boiling.

"Take your hands off those girls!" shouted Sister Christine.

"Yeah, take your hands off me pervert," said Janie, full of soapsuds and trying to straighten the collar on her costume.

"Wait, I can't see," said Hoshimi, squinty-eyed, trying to see through the water drops of her glasses while having Leo in a stranglehold. Then in sudden disbelief, everyone, brought to a standstill at the improbable sight of Sister Christine, so far from the classroom, frowning, standing in all her intractable hand-on-hip form, standing with Sister Carolyn who put her hand over her mouth to keep from laughing, standing next to Richard.

"Not one, not so much as a friendly handshake, between you, in those wet clothes," said Sister Christine, as if she were trying to count down to her calmer voice.

"Hoshimi, Hoshimi, you can unlock your arms and legs and let, Leo, go, now! He's beginning to turn blue!" said Sister Carolyn, followed by an outburst of laughter from all of us as Sister Carolyn covered her mouth for a second time, this time to hide a smile. "Girls, where did the rest of your heels go?"

"Heels?" questioned Sister Christine, looking at Sister Carolyn, "seriously?" Then she looked at Cassie, Hoshimi, Penny, and Janie and said, "Where did the rest of your clothes go?" raising her voice back up to the top of her throat.

"But we don't know where they fell off," answered Penny, meekly and to the original question of the missing heels while soapsuds dripped off her body.

"Oh, Lord is this some kind of test you're giving me?" shouted Sister Christine, "Gentlemen, I am especially shocked and disappointed in your behavior."

"Sister," pleaded Greg, Mike, and Bill.

"That's enough, Greg," said Richard, under his breath. Imploring us with a squeezed stare to realize if we were going to plead anything in front of Sister Christine, it had better be the fifth.

"I saw them walking around earlier dressed in their street clothes," said Sister Christine in her normal voice to Sister Carolyn and Richard.

"Girls, please tell me you didn't change your clothes in this parking lot," said Sister Carolyn.

"We changed at school," replied Hoshimi who was still having some trouble with her glasses.

"Good, this is a tight spot, but we can manage it," said Sister Carolyn.

"We can't let them walk or ride through the town underdressed like this," said Sister Christine. "How can we get them to the school and to their street clothes and space to dry without causing a public scene?"

"She's right, you're going to have to take my car," said Richard to Sister Carolyn.

"How is everyone going to fit in your small car?" questioned Sister Christine. "I drove up in it in the back seat, not much room back there."

"You're right, that's why I am going to give you my key so you and Sister Carolyn can drive the girls back to school. I'll walk back to the Academy with the boys and get a little more information," said Richard. "You are all going to have to breathe in girls and squeeze yourselves into my car. We can't take the risk of having you walk through town dressed the way you all dressed."

"But we didn't do anything wrong," said Penny.

Chapter 19

United in Fate

Soon after our successful carwash that brought in more than enough money for us to be in the town's spring festival, Cassie made me treasurer of the class funds. The longer the spring days, the longer I was spending time with Penny as well as Hoshimi, Janie, Greg Tarantino, Mike Redwood, Bill, Leo, and Dave at spring planning meetings run by Cassie. Although we had a sizable amount of money at our disposal, Cassie was disposing of it as if we had twice as much.

The Drama Festival part of the class competition is a collaborative form of fine art that uses live performers to present the experience of a real or imagined event before a live audience in the St. Gregory Catholic Academy's theater. The performers may communicate this experience to the audience through combinations of gesture, speech, song, music, or dance. Elements of design and stagecraft are used to enhance the physicality, presence, and immediacy of the experience.

However, Cassie's idea for the class's entry into the drama contest was one of the best-kept secrets at the Academy. So much so, it prompted a formal complaint by the other classes to reveal what we were planning. Since there was no requirement anywhere forcing any one class to admit what they were planning before they did it, according to Hoshimi, our class according to Cassie did not have to give up what Cassie saw as our shrewd competitive advantage. What I thought was lacking in courtesy on her part was to keep drama contest a top secret, Cassie refused to tell Greg Tarantino, Mike Redwood, Bill, Leo, Dave and me of what she was planning to do in the competition, reducing my role as class treasurer to being Cassie's walking wallet.

The class's culinary share of the planning for the Culinary Arts Festival competitions was pretty straight forward according to Cassie since Greg Tarantino, Mike Redwood, Bill, Leo, Dave and I could not cook well or as Cassie put it, cook at all. Based upon the lunches that were prepared every school day by Cassie, Penny, Hoshimi, and Janie, Cassie decided that Penny and Hoshimi had the best self-prepared lunches and would do well in the Culinary Arts Festival competitions if they prepared the entry themselves. Evidently, culinary comparing and contrasting at the school's lunch table where they all sat had been going on between them for years.

Penny first started giving me her extra dessert whenever she happened to have one. As we got to talking about food, she asked me if I would mind if she on occasion could start to cook me things to get my opinion. That is how I found out what an incredible chef she could be.

In this food finicky seaside town, most students in the Culinary Arts Festival shied away from anything to do with making clam chowder for fear they would surely disappoint the towns hardened New Englanders who were the last word on the subject of what makes a good clam chowder. I can't say that Penny thought twice about it. I do not believe that Penny thought about it at all, but Cassie thought together Penny, and Hoshimi might pull it off by giving the town's clam chowder's hardiest critics what they loved and loved to act professional about by being so critical. Seaside town pride might be able to tip the scales of the contest in our favor if it was good to great, Cassie thought, knowing Penny and Hoshimi never cooked anything that wasn't good to great.

They offered another choice of mussels. For dinner, they made a last-minute substituted of Nantucket Striped Bass for black sea bass and threw in a replacement of Chilean Sea bass which they plan to serve with lobster ravioli in a light cream sauce. Sautéed halibut they added for some reason, Brussels sprouts, and red smashed potatoes and also, for dessert a moist chocolate cake layered with dark chocolate mousse and coated with a hazelnut ganache. Crème Anglaise chopped toasted hazelnuts and a Pirouline lined with dark chocolate, a Chocolate Hazelnut Cake.

The Culinary competition of the Arts Festival takes place on the morning of the Festival. Some of the seaside town's best restaurateurs come to the school's improvised bistro to judge the entrees. Each class's entry is on the bistro's menu and can be requested throughout the day. Each class must prepare many their entrees ahead of time, and when they run out of the entry at the bistro, the entree is no longer available. The top award is best entrée followed by Soups, Chili & Chowders, and Desserts.

Chapter 20

Moon Empties to Illuminate the Darkness

It was a warm sunny shining late spring morning flooding a bright blue sky on the Saturday before the spring festival. The kind of morning dressed in a blue sky that brings the sound of birds singing through an open screened window. I hung around lying on the couch watching a baseball game on television as my little sister Katie was playing with her dolls on the coffee table.

The home team with red socks was playing out of town with a losing record against the team with black socks. The other team was running away with the score. I found myself thinking of Penny having given my head a break from thinking about Cassie when the phone suddenly rang.

The Sun They Called the Moon`

"Meet us in town at the bus stop," said Cassie, and she hung up the telephone.

My sister looked up towards me, and I look back at her. She was silent in astonishment that I would hold a phone for so long, still holding the phone in my hand; I wondered whether I should pretend to be still talking to someone. The phone rang in my hand bringing to an end that idea, but not the funny look of my little sister staring at me.

"Oh, don't bring your bike, but bring the class's checkbook and your wallet," said Cassie, and then Cassie hung up, again.

It didn't take as long as I thought it would to get to the town's bus stop. When I arrived there, Cassie was waiting along with Penny, Hoshimi, and Janie. They were dressed exactly alike, tailored and catered to the same style and that was typical. What was unfamiliar to me was the significant theme change at the sight of them all wearing long pants covering the bottom half of them. They also wore long loose raincoats that were open and went down over their knee, dark glasses, and had all their incredible free flowing hair stuffed into baseball caps. Penny waved and smiled as I approached. Hoshimi lifted up the non-prescription dark glasses off her nose, squinting in the sun, trying to figure out who I was. Janie looked at Cassie staring at me.

"You're late," Cassie said. "Why are you always late?" The bus arrived before I could think of something to say and Penny, Hoshimi, Janie, and Cassie walked on the bus and sat down, leaving the bus driver looking at me to pay the fair. He would not take a check. I slid next to Penny on the bus seat; she smiled, but across from Cassie and then Cassie looked threateningly at me as if I had done something wrong. I stared down at the bottom of Cassie's raincoat. Then she proclaimed rather sternly and unsparingly," It's going to rain, blockhead."

"Where are we all going, Cassie?" I asked, as the bus flying over a large bump made a loud thud and momentarily popped its passengers out of their seats.

"We are going down Frosty Valley passed Woodpecker Hill," said Cassie.

Going pass, Woodpecker Hill was like going to where all the bad things happen in the world that you can read about safe and secure the next morning online or in your newspaper or hear about on the radio driving to work or coming home or you can see on the six o'clock news. The other side of Woodpecker Hill according to the town wasn't any good and good for nothing. It is the place where murders happen, and the rapes happen. The other side of Woodpecker Hill was where the town needed it to be, somewhere over there where very horrible things can happen. The place some people can point to and say, that's terrible, and what a shame, but knowing it could never occur in the town they live in because it always happens there. I had no idea what Cassie was talking about, but Cassie, Penny, Hoshimi, and Janie having lived in the town all their lives, feared this other place.

"We need to write a pawnbroker a check for some of the equipment we need for The Drama Festival class competition," said Cassie.

The Pawnshop stood dilapidated as the sixth building on Chaplin Street next to a gutted storefront with the Mutual Plastic Film Company name, time-worn and barely visible, painted on it and next to it in the backstreet alleyway.

The pawnshop had a filthy old sign that stated, Henry Bergman and Edna Purviance, proprietors, in the front window, but it was a sign from long ago, and they might have been the owners once, but not now. It was just a not now kind of space.

It was an awkward space to be trapped in and even a more hostile place for Penny, Hoshimi, Janie, and Cassie who showed signs of worry. The whole street had a foul stench of beer and urine and the sight of some of the men looking at Penny, Hoshimi, Janie, and Cassie made me uneasy.

The pawnshop had a huge inventory. It was crammed with used athletic gear, old tools, and old stereos, the store owner must have spent a lot of time and money shelving all this, and sorting items, displaying them on different stands in glass cases, and having to monitor each customer to prevent shoplifting I thought.

The shadowy silhouettes of men leering stunk up the space with their foul smelling smokes that filtered through the dank mustiness of the shop. We walked by old toasters, scratched-up 20-year-old TVs, and worn-out sports gear piled into cardboard boxes, and the store began to look more like a rummage sale or flea market until you got to the vintage Harley Davidson motorcycle.

There was just enough light to see in front of you barely. Let alone make clear the gray outlines of the beer bellies, unshaven faces or the direction of the smell of greasy hair. You could feel their eyes leering in an unpleasant, malicious, and lascivious way from the dark shadows on the back of your neck. It was worse for Cassie, Penny, Janie, and Hoshimi. They did not think it necessary to remove their dark sunglasses to see well out of an abundance of precaution to prevent someone from actually recognizing them.

We followed Cassie in a straight line through a narrow path between the nooks and crannies of the space. Hoshimi bounced blind off Janie's back and started stumbling helplessly into objects, and before she was about to walk into one of the men, I quickly grabbed her hand, turning her and held it to keep her by my side to guide her.

The counter of the shop was higher than the average person I guess for security. A customer would only be able to hold up a hand to offer up the hocking or fencing of what they held. There was a wooden screen between the door and the counter for the customers' privacy. Cassie reached up shoulder length to a nickel-plated silver call bell with a wooden base and for the aesthetics banged it repeatedly until a wooden screen between the doors opened. A pear-shaped man blew cigar smoke at her dark glasses.

"I'm Cassie, you told me over the phone that you can supply me with everything I need," said Cassie, refusing to take notice or shrink back, out of pain or fear over the smoke he blew.

"As I told you over the phone, Slim Sister, it depends," he said, conveying to her diminutiveness and his condescending attitude. "Do you have the scratch?"

"Will," said Cassie. "Get the check ready for this nice guy but before I hand it to you let me get this straight. You will make the delivery at St. Gregory Catholic Academy School's theater next Saturday." He turned and looked at one of his guys. "And you will set it all up on stage as we agreed over the phone, right?"

"I don't get it Slim, I used to be an altar boy," he said, wooly-eyed with his cigar unbalancing about his lower lip.

"Forget it; you will set it all up for us, right?" Cassie said.

"Yeah, yeah, Slim, we'll set it all up on stage," he said.

"Good," Cassie said, and turned to me, waited, lifted up her glasses, and showed her wide eyes, saying; "Give him the check, what is with you?"

I handed the guy a large check with one hand while still holding Hoshimi's hand with the other and in a moment, the amount we delivered to him just about emptied out all the money we raised. I still did not have any idea of what the big school secret was and what she was planning to do for the Drama Festival. As we all walked out to leave, following Cassie in a straight line through the narrow, smelly, nook and cranny of glint, wink, gleam, squint, gape and grin and leering gazes from dirty looking old men. I was wondering about jail time and if there would be any for me when they find out Cassie made me write a check to these shady characters.

I was also wondering where they would find our dead bodies.

"Hey, hey," one of the men called out wanting us to stop walking.

"Ignore them," said Janie, under her breath. "Walk faster; don't make eye contact, no eye contact."

I began feeling Hoshimi slowly, clenching my hand in hers like a vise grip, slowly crunching it as if she was a kitchen appliance crushing cans. She folded my arm into hers. She was walking me out faster.

"Hey, Slim, hey, "continued the man, calling out to us to stop.

Cassie stopped abruptly, causing us all to stop and bump into each other. She turned, put her hands thunderously on her hips, and with a scornful look towards the person, shouted, "What!"

"You guys are pretty flaky. You know that don't ya," he said.

"Huh," Cassie said, and Penny, Janie, and Hoshimi followed her out into the sunlight where Hoshimi let my hand go.

Chapter 21

The Moon Rises Before Our Eyes

The Friday before the Spring Festival after we traded back notebooks in the corner of the classroom, Cassie asked me to go with Greg, Mike, Bill, Leo, and Dave to Janie's house. After Cassie, Penny, Hoshimi, and Janie finished their final mystery rehearsal for the drama part of the arts festival competition. I was to bring my wallet and the class's checkbook and go with them to the farmer's market in town before it closes. She would call and did when they finished rehearsal. When we arrived, everyone was in street clothes. The girls were waiting for us on the steps of Janie's house.

"Well, aren't you going to say I'm late?" I asked, wanting to say it before she beat me to it, just one time.

"No, why would I say that?" replied Cassie, trying on naïvetés and offering resistance, cheerfully. But like a shoe that didn't quite fit, she rose to furrow her eyebrows at me. "Hoshimi is carrying the list of ingredients that Penny put together. We need the exact amounts that Hoshimi calculated we would need to make the entrées for the culinary contest tomorrow as well as what we will need for the bistro when we win. It is a lot of stuff, and we would like help in carrying it all back to Penny's house that has the double oven in her kitchen."

"I buy fruits, vegetables, and eggs at the market all the time and know the grocer pretty well," said Penny. "I just love their bananas," she continued, enthusiastically with lively interest. "They call me their banana girl."

"Banana girl," I said. Penny had spiked my interest. Then I caught a stay away glance from Hoshimi that asked me, are you really going to go there?

"They really like me at the Farmers Market, and they let me sit down and eat all the bananas I want right there for free. They have such big bananas," said Penny, adding to my curiosity.

Both Janie and Penny's house were close to town, and it didn't take us long before we were all in town. When we arrived in front of the open aired Farmers Market, we were warmly, but peculiarly greeted by the grocer with an unusual order of words.

"There's my banana girl, and she brought all her friends, and have you come to eat more bananas?" asked the grocer.

"No one is going to eat bananas," said Hoshimi, curtly.

"Aw, that's a shame," replied the grocer.

"No?" questioned Penny, sweetly with a big smile. "We are here because we will be entering tomorrow's spring food competition," Penny continued. "We want to win and need your help to get us some things. Hoshimi, show him the list." The grocer took the list and began to study it with one hand, and then started to rub the thin stubble of his chin with the other and then he looked up and back down at them.

"It's going to take a little time to put together. Are you sure, you don't want to eat a banana while you wait?" asked the grocer.

"No one is going to eat any bananas," said Hoshimi. The grocer shrugged his shoulders in unexpected resignation.

"I don't see why we...," said Penny.

"Clam up, Penny," said Cassie.

"Button up," said Hoshimi.

"Put the banana away, Penny," said Janie, all cutting off Penny at once in mid-sentence, smiling politely at the grocer, and then biting their lip and looking away.

"Ok, you kids wait here," said the grocer, "I'm going to play a little trick and pass around this list to everyone in the market, and we'll pretend that you're a fancy restaurant in town and it's a rush emergency. Nothing's too good for the banana girl." Penny sweetly leaned forward with her chest and with an engaging smile; she had complete celebrity ownership of the town's entire open-air market. I passed the time sitting in the marketplace going over the class's checkbook with Cassie and watching Penny pout as she stared at a bunch of large bananas while some strange people who worked nearby looked at her pleasantly, eagerly waiting to see if she would eat a banana.

The big grocer marched out to us with five little grocers behind him holding large paper bags of gourmet food ingredients usually reserved for the better restaurants in town. "Here you go, banana girl. You will always have friends here to help you," said the grocer.

"Thank you, thank you," said Penny.

"Great," said Cassie. "How much do we owe you?" He handed her his handwritten itemized bill.

"Remember, you have the best ingredients in the place, first class all the way and I gave a twenty percent discount," said the grocer, reassuringly. Cassie looked over the bill.

"It looks fine and fair," Cassie said and smiled approvingly at the grocer. "Pay the man," she continued, handing me the bill. I wrote him a check that emptied out our checking account. We followed Cassie, Penny, Hoshimi, and Janie to Penny's house carrying grocery bags while Penny complained how hungry she was for a banana.

Once at Penny's house, music began to play throughout the kitchen to start the cooking party. Everyone moved in an outward demonstration of playfulness as we held lively our humor while moving to the backbeat of a song.

Hoshimi took charge of all distribution of assignments and measurement, leaving Penny as head chef. It was an enormous kitchen with a long counter table island. Hoshimi lined us up on one side of the table island while she parceled out ingredients in exact measurement to us from the other side. Everyone had a knife and cutting board and began chopping up their ingredients. Hoshimi then took the measured chopped up ingredients to Penny to add to the pot, pan, and oven as she deemed fit.

Then I saw that even in a single piece of fish the colors of love are worn. In the yellows, reds, and purples that are all the colors of the dawn. Where sea birds take wing to soar, where the wind alternately presses them back, on the unremitting shore, where the twisted shifting wind in sunlight, spins madly, lifting wings, until their want and their desire are left below them and are no more.

Chapter 22

Painted Wagons Return

The next morning that was once the dawn, before sleep was gone, and the sun sets to rise. I awoke to the sound of songbirds singing soft and low through the gentle trees that grow, in the delicate and soothing breezes that blow, so much greener than the sky.

Far beneath my window, the morning's bright glow spread, embracing the seaside, reaching the meadow-grass fields, and filling the many wildflowers with a sunshine pleasing the senses by revealing the many multi-colored flowers awakening in countless variety sensations in front of me. On this beautiful day, in a day made for everyone, an unidentifiable peace came to be like the feeling of Cassie and Penny resting on me.

My legs rush to rise and fall, pass the sunlight patterns on my wall, pass my cat contently soaking up the sun. Just a minute and I only had one, down to the stair, down to the floor, down to the kitchen, and down to the door to my bike and down the street. Down to the beat of my legs once more, rushing to rise and rushing to fall, pass the sunlight awakening patterns on drowsy resident walls.

I continued to peddle and glide without a care through the morning current of the air that was high enough to make the trees sway. Not much can I say, you see I saw her last night, yes I saw her standing there. I flashed on to last night's images still swimming in my head of her flour powdered covered dimples, dancing on her face.

Her unrelenting chase to chain reactions of tickling bomb attacks, enlivened by music, lively, and cheerful, making the clock run into the night too fast and far for anyone to notice or care. Her cheeks flush through the evening, her emerald eyes flashing wide to both our sound and the locking of our sight, and then shyly turning away from me. Her shrinking smile falls into me.

The Sun They Called the Moon`

Light is shifting in the sun. Every second I passed through is like a minute less with you. Passed the flowers reaching out to speak to passersby as they reach their peak, rushing to the eye. Light is shifting on everyone.

Dragon kite tails hover above sea sparks below an azure sky, wheel, and turn, spin and fly. Be watchful my friend of how high you fly.

She may not know.

Artists walking through the seaside town, paint on the walls and the pavements, drawing surprising statements. Marionettes once whittled and painted on hooks, feed sensitivity to both greed, and crooks.

Marionettes dance, and dangle above the planks, stepping in time to the minstrels' pranks, tapping to the wooden beat, dancing there at his feet.

The Sun They Called the Moon`

Grocery clerks quickly recognizing me, all waved welcome back to me, speeding down the street and pedaling faster with my feet, I wave.

I felt a warming feeling settling on my shoulder as the morning sun was getting older. Racing between the meadows, I had a vision in the shade. When the sun sets to rise caravans unidentified to man fly through the once was dawn, before sleep is gone, out of a tinker's sky. Painted by hand, ride out of the sun, pulled forward by Dobbins and seen by no one until they land and arrive as an unexpected tide.

When I rode into the parking lot of the school, it was empty, and the wet morning's dew was still low on the lawn, filling all the air with the smell of the fresh green cut grass mowed the night before. The first songbirds through the black wood elm and Japanese pagoda trees were singing songs I never heard before.

The hallways were eerily silent as I walked down them, but I didn't care. I eyed a judge arriving early for the culinary competition, and I didn't care. I didn't sleep last night, and I didn't care. All I cared about was seeing her again because I knew she did care and knowing this I took a chance and if I was right it might be all right, she might be here, surprisingly, earlier too. Because the feeling, when I was with her last night was all right, it felt right.

Penny sat with a cheerful self-complacency in her smile as she sat in a white straw chair in white leg stockings rising above her knees to the upper portions of her thighs. The full body of Penny's sequin hair effortlessly poured from the top of her head off her shoulders. Attractive within two slender deep blue fabric streams of her halter-top, her lush, round breasts cleaved together in front of me in perfect harmony.

How much cleavage to leave in and how much to leave out she clearly achieved with a natural ease. Two straight deep blue pieces of silk fabric branched out vertically down over each prominent round firm breast from her stiff white collar, flowing directly down to the skirt of her waitress outfit, carrying the blue color downward. Interrupted only by a white lacy ruffle and the fluent likeness of her skin on her upper thigh.

I thought I would take a second look to see what I could see and I shared her in a double dose with nobody there but me. She didn't drink a lot, but she drank me into wonderland where we spent the time giggling and laughing. However, know this if you are able or leave while you still can. Love is unstable when built on what must come and go with the wind and sand.

After a while, I heard the increasing activity from the Hall as the campus was starting to come alive and I said to Penny, "I think we need to get to the bistro" and she responded by slipping one brown shoe over her white nylon stocking.

"I hope this zipper doesn't get stuck again," Penny said, leaning over to reach under the hem of her hot pants skirt. "We don't need any fashion police today," she continued, as she pulled the zipper to lower the folded hem, dropping it, about eight inches, and she smiled and looked up at me. "We had to promise Sister Carolyn and Richard, no high heels just the school's clodhoppers and the hemline right above the knee." Standing straight up, she slid her index fingers down from her white collar toward her skirt over her breasts, in one motion vertically extending, and widening the two pieces of fabric flowing down her chest to cover every beautiful curve of her breast. "Oh well, easy off, easy on, thanks to Hoshimi and her sewing machine," Penny continued, and she paused to smile. "How do I look?"

"You look fantastic," I said, smiling back at her.

"Thank you," Penny replied, looking up at me and blushing and then I did too.

"Let's go," I said, taking her hand like it was a flower, "I have a great feeling about all the work we did last night," I continued, briefly leading her out the door and into the hall. "I think we have a good chance of winning." I let her hand go, and she placed her hand gently on the other at her chest, her eyes met mine. Then her eyes gave the impression of having disappeared in her blush, making way for a happy consenting smile.

The campus had come alive with activity; it soon turned loud. The morning's festivity was at its peak at the bistro as the contest for the best-prepared meal was underway. Hoshimi came running in wearing her waitress outfit, followed speedily by Cassie and Janie in their street clothes when Penny and I arrived together.

"Where were you," said Cassie to me, angrily.

"But you just got here," I said.

"No, Sherlock, "I've been here all morning," snapped Cassie, stepping between Penny and me, with her right leg fully extended, and pointing at me in her shorts and sneaker. "Aren't you supposed to be with the perverts?"

"Speaking of them, here they are now," said Janie, motioning with her head to Cassie to look over her shoulder as Greg Tarantino, Mike Redwood, Bill, Leo, and Dave walked in.

"Hello, ladies and madam," said Greg Tarantino, looking at me. "I called your house, and someone sounding half asleep told me you must have already left, so for some reason, you operate on less sleep than the rest of us?" he questioned.

"Did they announce anything yet?" asked Leo.

"No," answered Hoshimi. "It should not be too much longer I hope. I'll go and find out," and she disappeared into the crowded bistro.

"It better not take long," said Bill. "I don't want to waste all this time waiting for them when I could be checking the rest of the spring festival out."

"Today's the day," said Mike Redwood, speaking to Cassie. "So are you going to finally tell us what's going on with the Drama Festival like you said you would last night?"

"Not yet," said Cassie. "It has to be a total surprise if we are going to get an edge with the Drama Festival judging panel."

"Did everything come in this morning for us?" asked Penny, wide-eyed and not afraid to use her natural voice that chirps out words in delightfully high tones. "Did they set things up like we asked them to?"

"I don't know, yet. Don't worry," said Cassie. "Things are going to get crazy around here when we win this thing, and it will even get crazier when we win the Drama Festival award. Remember we have been rehearsing this for months and the last run through went perfect so we can't lose. I promise everything will be ready when we meet up this afternoon. Janie and I will be able to handle it by ourselves while you and Hoshimi are passing out our killer award winning foods to the bistro customers and besides, the guys will be around for back-up until we get back here."

"Don't you think its time to tell them what we are going to do? After all, it is their class too.

Cassie," said Penny. Janie pulled Cassie and Penny over to the side.

"We kept them in the dark this far," replied Cassie.

"Which has got to be embarrassing to them," quibbled Janie, shaking her head. "I would think they are an embarrassment to their entire gender, no surprise there, not at all. These guys are way too easy to fool; I am talking fooled like a bunch of monkeys. They already know how to drool, hey, and look how easy it is to make them drool uncontrollably from the mouth. I'm right, am I right?"

"Janie's right. They are way too predictable and telling them now would only give them too many things to talk about, we can't take a chance. They give the girls in the classes we compete against way too much information as it is, I mean all they have to do is look at them twice and ask." said Cassie. "Besides, they waited all this time without us telling them what we were doing. They can wait a few hours more; it won't kill them to wait a little longer."

There was an uproar of applauds that went through the bistro and into the hall, followed by the low fading murmur of moans and Hoshimi bursting out of the crowd towards us.

"We won; we won at our first time at bat, and we hit a home run," said Hoshimi, gasping through words, jumping up and down. Everyone started to congratulate each other.

"Wait, which award?" I had asked before the room went still.

"But whatever do you mean, Will," replied Cassie, her voice dripping with sarcasm, putting her hands on her hips and giving me a snarky smile. "You can be so out of it; we won them all."

I looked over to Hoshimi who had dislodged her glasses but held her open smile. She nodded to me. Everyone roared in cheers. Hoshimi continued jumping up and down. The glasses fell off her head, but she flashed a smile I haven't seen in a while and said, "But Will," shouting over the cheers. "Isn't it wonderful? Isn't it wondrous? We have never lost together as a team. Can you believe it? I can't believe we keep doing this. The other classes are furious. They hate our guts!"

Chapter 23

The Land of the Glass Pennywhistles

After a short time had passed from the surreal and unbelievable way things had turned out, I decided to check out the brightly colored festival booths that were set up around the school. Whereas Greg Tarantino, Mike Redwood, Bill, Leo, and Dave were busy checking out the female underclassmen for who might be next year's early blooms. We agreed to meet back at the bistro for lunch. I was determined to enjoy the festival, so I dragged my sleep-deprived mind out a side door. I was now able to spend a peaceful morning at the Drama and Culinary Arts Spring Festival. It felt good to get back out into the cooler air.

The campus began to fill up with people. The festival relievers looked happy to be able to stretch their feet and necks once again. They showed little care to having arrived from the packed part of the campus's main road by feeder lines, drawing people from the town's main road where area visual artists were selling off their art. The visual arts in the seaside town grabbed much of the limelight as anything else at the festival. This was strikingly apparent at the Artists Pavilion in town that was filled to capacity and overflowing. The feeder lines were working at keeping the foot traffic congestion on the main road moving in and out of town. The campus drew people out of the town with crafts of exotic fabrics, silks, burlap, and tie-dyes. Artisans and exhibitors came from up and down the coast displaying their unique, custom, handcrafted merchandise. The campus with its flowering trees drifting in pink petals on the breeze became an oasis of shade during the day, and a beacon of firefly twinkling lights illuminating later in the night.

The "Global Bazaar" featuring indigenous imported products from around the world was located in a vibrant, old-world style circular market with a juggler's stage at the center. There were strawberry fair festival marketplace booths, multi-colored in tones of red filled with fresh strawberries just picked from fields off the vines and small strawberry shortcakes were being passed out for about a dime.

An entire area was devoted to kinetic sculptors and bicycle daredevils presenting unique, pedal-powered contraptions on a track for performance exhibits. Each of their vehicles was an oversized and unusual invention, entirely designed and handmade by the rider/artist. Some of the unique designs required four riders to operate, while others are designed for one individual.

I returned about two hours later and asked, "Did you guys check anything out besides girls?"

"Nope, there was not too much else to see," replied Greg Tarantino, sipping out the bottom of a bottle of Coca-Cola.

"The girl's freshman class had ice, though," said Bill.

"The girls in the Junior Class had strawberry cake," said Leo.

"The girls in the eighth grades had chocolate bananas with more chocolate than banana," said Dave.

"Your joking, all you've been doing is eating?" I asked.

"What else is there to do around here," said Mike Redwood.

"Yeah, we're sampling food," said Leo.

"And now it's time to sample the girls in their waitress's outfits at the bistro café," said Greg Tarantino.

"The get-ups Cassie, Hoshimi, Penny, and Janie, wore at the car wash were incredibly hot," said Mike Redwood. We walked to the end of a long line. The line, for the most part, was full of happy smiling young boys from the Academy, all having a pleasant feeling of the ludicrous, waiting to get in. "Even with their outfits toned down a bit," continued Mike Redwood. "Cassie, Hoshimi, Penny, and Janie will still look like they belong on the cover of a teen magazine, but when the other girls in the other classes found out what they were wearing, it was like they all had to play follow the leader and not be out braved."

"It's going to be great this year, I can't wait to see what the other girls are going to be wearing today," said Bill.

"I have a coupon," said Greg Tarantino.

"What, did you think that the costumes would be less if you had a coupon?" said Dave.

"I waited in line for twenty minutes," said Greg Tarantino, "and all we get is a free tea and some pasta. It wasn't worth the wait."

The Sun They Called the Moon`

"You don't have to go you know," I said.

"No way, are you crazy, not before we steal a peek at those short waitress's skirts and low cut necklines that are strutting all that stuff up and down and all around in there," said Greg Tarantino.

"And not one of them from what I've been told needs to stuff," said Mike Redwood.

"Totally," said Bill, "you just don't volunteer for the job if you don't have the right paraphernalia. This is what they do when the boob fairy arrives. It's like a coming-out party for boobs."

"You got that right," I said, seeing all the girls running free and finally out of reach of the outstretched hands of the religious whacko sexuality police.

"Yeah, this is where they are first displayed in all their glory," said Dave.

"I wonder if they're going to be as hot as they were at the car wash," said Mike Redwood.

"Hey, it's Greg Tarantino and his sidekicks. Get over here, you guys. Congrats, on bringing home the bacon as I like to say in food class and thanks for stopping by. A table for six today?" asked Debbie, emitting an attractive phosphorescent smile. "Oh, wait, hold on, what do you think about this outfit, I made it myself, doesn't it look totally fantabulous on me?" She spun around. She had a very tight white blouse on and it went up to her neck with puffy shoulders and a thin red bow tie, large blue cuffs and a very short dress, long leg stockings and brown shoes. "Aren't I cute, Will?"

She was very cute.

"Totally," I said. "You have certainly a large crowd in the bistro. The place is jam-packed solid.

"Totally, look at all these people waiting to get in," said Debbie, gushing. "We are raking in so much money it's getting hard to keep it all in the cash register. Sister Christine has had to empty it a few times already. Over there is the end of the line, come on," and she led us to the end of the line. "Oh, just so you know, the only thing we have left is pasta and tea, but the water is free and all you can drink. Just pay in advance."

"We have a ticket," said Greg Tarantino, as if it was some great deal. He handed her the ticket while I paid her.

"Ok, guys, hang out here, and your turn will be coming up soon," Debbie said.

"Boy, she's a high-strung girl," said Mike Redwood, as Debbie walked away and turned to go into the bistro. The soon that Debbie spoke of was about forty-five minutes long. We stood outside waiting that long until she finally let us in.

"Oh welcome to our bistro," said Penny, her body alone was worth the wait. She had a dazzling smile and made an awesome server. Penny put the other class servers to shame and seemed to beam here differently much more than in class. "Thank you so much for stopping by to see us today," she continued, passing out the cutlery to each one of us.

Without any debate, if they gave an award for best costume design Penny and Hoshimi would have won that as well. It didn't hurt that the two of them looked like they could be on the cover of Teen Fashion. They did make an excellent sight.

In the end, because of the long line, we were all forced out quickly to get the next customers in. So we inhaled the pasta and tea in about ten minutes. After, we all were feeling disappointingly hungry.

"Well, what do you guys want to do," said Mike Redwood. "I thought we'd check out the jugglers."

"Lame," said Greg Tarantino.

"How about the fortune tellers?" suggested Mike Redwood.

"Lame," said Bill.

"The pirate with the parrot, they're selling model remote controlled pirate ships," said Mike Redwood.

"Lame," said Leo.

"You guys go ahead and try to do whatever you want to do as normally as you can do it," I said. "I'm pretty beat from last night. I'm going to wander to the theater and check out the Drama Festival and chill out.

Chapter 24

The Flowers in Your Heart

I was also curious about what the other classes were doing for the Drama Festival competition. I picked-up one of the programs over by the raffle booth and looked at it. One of the classes had a string quartet consisting of two violins, a viola, and a cello that was playing right now, soon to be followed by a jazz fusion ensemble. Then one of the classes will be doing Woody Allen's one-act play, God, a satire on a Greek playwright that quickly proceeds into an utterly ruthless comedy according to the blurb in the program. I scanned my eyes down to the bottom of the program to our class entry, reading the description, "not available at printing." This can't be a good omen, I thought. I walked down the hall, pushing one of the theater doors open. The theater had plenty of seats. I sat down in the fourth row to strains of Ravel's string quartet ending in my ear.

The chair was comfortable. I slid down into it to hear jazz-fusion. I close my eyes to rest them for what I thought would be a minute, but when I opened them again, I saw something entirely different on stage. A drama with actors laughing. I noticed that many more people had come to the theater to watch two men dressed in Shakespearian costume wager while flipping coins.

Competition is not their purpose. Although the actors are talking to one another, they are not speaking. No communication is being achieved.

One of the players wants to know how it is possible for a coin to land heads up almost a hundred times in a row. They are not worried about the money, but one of the player's worries about the implications. There is no back and forth since the players are interchangeable. There is no up or down since the players appear to follow one another. It is not the world existing as a thing or occurring in fact; and I closed my eyes again, for what I hoped would be for another minute. So went my afternoon, catching glimpses of the performances until Greg Tarantino, Mike Redwood, Bill, Leo, and Dave sat around me in a crowded theater.

The Sun They Called the Moon`

The play that was about to start was "Little Women." It is a story based on the novel by Louisa May Alcott and tells a story of four girls, Meg, Jo, Beth, and Amy, as they grow to adulthood in Civil War Era New England. The girls bear misfortune, deprivations, and eventually a tragic loss, but their courageousness, the love for each other, and the enduringness of their family bond pulling them together instead of apart. Greg Tarantino, Mike Redwood, Bill, Leo, and Dave got the weird idea it was about something else.

The four women in the story may have endured hardships and privations, and eventually even a tragic loss, but it was nothing like what the audience had to take during the hour of this play's poor performance. I had lost track of time and my program.

It was a relief that the breakdown of the stage between performances this time did not take as long as it usually did. I began to feel hopeful about the next performance when I spotted percussion instruments surrounded by a wall of massive Marshall Amplifiers, big enough to be loud enough to wake everyone up out of the last performance that put everyone to sleep.

It was as if everyone who went to the Drama Festival competition were on a mind-numbing pricey vacation and were looking for something to do that would justify the time, effort, and cost of the effort of having gone. The murmur from people in what was now a sold-out theater with a standing-room crowd packed to the back got louder with expectation. They were feeling they have been waiting long enough and it was time to get on with it and to the awards presentation. Soon people began to stamp their feet for whoever was next just to get things moving again and whoever was next had better be good.

As the stomping in time began to peak, I thought they better get out there to stop the crowd from throwing things on the stage before they start. I began to sweat. The theater did not have air conditioning. I became uneasy, thinking what they might throw at the next act after they start.

Then in something regarded as likely never to happen, Cassie, followed by Hoshimi, Penny, and Janie walked out on the stage and surprised the crowd, putting them into a stunned silence. They stepped out in long sharp heels in the outfits they wore at the car wash, but set to overdrive, revealing every curve. They were downright, hard-hitting, wielding a posture and attitude as if it was a katana on fire and had no problem pointing that mental attitude directly at the crowd. Still, it was not hot enough to unfreeze the chill of taken on a situation that no one believes you could possibly master.

I sat there amazed as Janie walked confidently to sit behind the drums. Hoshimi wore the same revealing blue costume as her band mates but added a touch of character from a J. R. R. Tolkien novel. Hoshimi wore a hat she sewed together in the same Academy blue color of her stage costume and school uniform, but unlike a witch's hat and its point, the point folded over to one side in what was an accurate reproduction of the hat worn by Gandalf, the wizard.

Penny and Cassie carried electric guitars in front of the microphones as if they had done this walk all their lives. Nevertheless, you could have cut the atmosphere of the silence of the crowd with a knife. They were expecting excessive failure. Finally, they were going to see it.   It all had me wondering. Did Cassie and the class take on a situation we could not master, finally doing too many things at the same time, and not succeeding by taken on more responsibilities than can be managed?

Janie tapped twice on the drumsticks. The sound, active and energetic, stabbed and clipped through the silent air. Then a wall of sound blasted from the stage in intricate jazz melodies as well as complex R&B arrangements with a shuffling beat moving towards more intense sections, which intertwined in short musical flourishes.

However, it wasn't until the sweet juices flowed in the clean bridges of a screaming guitar lead from Hoshimi's surprisingly quick fingers, near the end of their first song that everyone started to realize they were band mates who played like solid pros and knew what they were doing. After the closing vocal lines of desperation in their first song left the listener questioning whether the song is praising or bashing "love's" familiar boy-loves-girl relationship songs. The large assembled crowd of listeners jumped to their feet with a roar and ecstatic faces, hooting, shouting, and whistling, stamping their feet, and clapping their hands in approval and admiration.

The songs were straightforward with themes of rebelliousness and not fading away. Lyrically, the songs were in the majority performed with an unwavering high energy and were quite intense. In any case, the songs were original and played in an excellent rhythm backbeat to back up the vocals

"Ah, hi," said Cassie, sounding timid in front of the large crowd. "We are She Wolf," she said. Then the crowd roared loudly in welcoming approval. "Unfortunately, we realized too late that some of our equipment hadn't been delivered, but that doesn't seem to matter," she continued, through the feedback from her mike and instinctively knowing saying this to an already enthusiastic revved up crowd would make them louder.

"Let me introduce you all to the band. On drums we have Janie!" Janie banged on the drums and cymbals for the crowd. Janie wasn't a flashy drummer. Janie had a cool about her when she played that fed into her confidently keeping a steady beat. Wild and spastic with double-kick drums, to grinding out blast beats, she mastered the intricate jazz melodies as well as the complex R&B arrangements.

"And that's Penny on bass!" Cassie continued. Penny played a tight riff on her bass, swinging the bass guitar off her extending high heel slim leg to approving cheers. Penny had the bonus of a very dynamic rhythm with her bass guitar. Her sound had a bouncy bass and guitar line for very assertive vocals, and she played with ease, but she was undoubtedly the backbone of their entire sound. A slap bass sound that fueled her band with deeply melodic, flawless bass parts, Penny played it like a lead instrument just when the songs called for it, creating a powerful, booming sound that often overshadowed with thundering beats. Her rotating bass line progressing into a jazzy fusion piece fit very well with Cassie's indignant melodic, layered vocals that sang about destiny and immortality.

"And on lead guitar, we have Hoshimi!" Cassie continued, and Hoshimi jumped in with a rapid riff. When Hoshimi's guitar jumps into the song midway through, it seems to change it almost completely. She brings the features of slide and position shift, followed by a tap, then string-skips the pentatonic scales. This last ability gave the band a cool flash burst riff to have in their armory. Hoping the crowd likes the spicy blues sound. Here, they had an impressive guitar assault. They had through Hoshimi's fast mid-tempo numbers, the skill, and talent to ruthlessly an emotionally hit the sweet spot to add interest by giving an ear-twisting minor and major sound, typical of a great lead guitarist.

"My name is Cassie on vocals and sometimes rhythm guitar. I don't know how well I am doing singing in front of you all today. I'm sort of winging it," Cassie said, knowing she would get the thunderous applause that followed. "So that's that, we're gonna do one more. Is that cool?" The crowd grew louder. "We just have a few songs, and we finished the last one about an hour ago. I know some of you were looking for more, but we will play our hearts out for you. Ready!"

The Sun They Called the Moon`

One thing about all good singers and Cassie was one of them is the ability to create a state of temporary mental surrender and to the altered consciousness to what they inspire. The other weird thing is the unmasking response a singer can arouse once we have recovered our senses. It is as if they have pulled us into loving them, got into our hard-wired head, and located vulnerability in us that we long ago thought we had numbed out of our lives. This is why every time it happens when we fall in love with the singer that moves us into the song it is like being a teenager.

Perhaps this is why Cassie, being a young girl was so powerful, so fearless on that stage. Cassie sang with a rawness that deepened the ache and grit in her powerhouse cries and moans. It is not about how pretty the voice is. It is about believing that the voice is telling the truth. Dirt-bowl yelps, bluesy street howls, and most melancholy tunes do not succumb to sentimentality. It is a voice like smoke, from cigar to incense, full of wonder, admiration, and affection. Free from the prissy rules, unchain by sentiments laid down by the schoolmarms, unchain and through the fourth wall that is up in the audience's face and says, "I dare you to think I'm just clowning around here."

Unprepared for an encore, Cassie, Hoshimi, Penny, and Janie had to repeat their first song for an audience that didn't mind. Hoshimi unexpectedly opened up the middle of the tune as a jazz musician with a much longer improv guitar riff. Cassie and Penny turned to face Hoshimi to see the cords on the stem of her guitar to follow her lead with their own playing in this new extended version of their first song that rocked the crowd for about twenty minutes.

After their concert was over, Greg Tarantino, Mike Redwood, Bill, Leo, Dave and I went backstage to join, Cassie, Hoshimi, Penny, and Janie who were trying to catch their breath, soaked in their sweat. I ran to get and handed them each a bottle of water. They took it leaning and panting against the brick wall of the backstage while the crowd showed no signs letting up on their clapping. They began to slip off their heels from their aching feet.

"That's it, we can't go back out there," said Cassie. Richard, Sister Carolyn, and Sister Christine went up to them.

"You guys were crowd pleasers," said Sister Carolyn.

"I'll say one thing about you," said Sister Christine. "If anyone knows how to stir a crowd up it would be you, people."

"You may have angered the Drama Festival events committee with your camouflage and secrecy of what you had planned," said Richard, "but I think it worked, now if the judges agree with that screaming crowd, you might have the Drama Festival judges handing you the Best in Performance Award."

"You know," said Sister Christine "I would have pulled the plug on this peep show, and this blasted music if you two didn't stop me. For the life of me, I can't understand why it seems they had fewer clothes on stage than they do off stage."

"Like we said, it's stagecraft, all lighting, angle, and heels," replied Sister Carolyn.

"You two," said Sister Christine, "You have to remind me to edit the student dress code. We must ban students from ever wearing high heels on campus. They are a filthy influence. I mean on them."

"Sure thing, Sister," replied Richard, looking at Sister Carolyn with neither one of them intending to do it.

"Hey," said Greg Tarantino, "The judges are walking on to the stage." The crowd showed no signs of quieting down and then all of a sudden you heard nothing at all. It was less than a minute before the silence erupted into a thunderous roar and since I didn't listen to any, oh not them again, murmurings, I couldn't be all that sure.

"We won, we won," shouted Mike Redwood, running towards us with Bill, Leo, and Dave. The judges couldn't ignore the performance and the crowd's enthusiastic reaction to it.

"Good," said Penny, "I'm so tired of being stuck inside. Can we get out of this crowded space? I don't think I've been outdoors all day."

"You said it," said Janie. "My feet are killing me."

"Mine too," said Hoshimi.

"I want to walk on the soft grass," said Cassie, looking at me. I looked back and began walking away. Cassie followed and ran up to me with heels in hand followed by Hoshimi, Penny, and Janie in their blackening white nylon stockings feet carrying their heels. Greg Tarantino, Mike Redwood, Bill, Leo, and Dave walked with them.

As we exited a back door, we were immediately hit by a fresh burst of colder welcoming air. We all hurried down the stairs quietly in a daze. The only sounds were from the amplifiers still ringing in our ears. We quickly walked across the parking lot. Away from the garish street lights and over to the other side of a small hill where Cassie, Hoshimi, Penny, and Janie rolled off and tossed away their stockings to feel the earth and the grass under their feet, following into an open field of wildflowers, we all were silhouetted by the crescent moon.

Once in the middle of the field, I stopped and lay down on the ground, down into it, lying there to feel the living earth on my back, head, feet, and hands. Then everyone stopped where they stood and fell with their backs up against the ground with Cassie and Penny falling next to me. We all looked up at the starry sky. The ringing in our ears faded to the soothing sounds of the summer field.

The school year had officially ended, leaving us with summer ahead with summer homework and nights and days spent at the beach. I would continue to get abrupt telephone calls from Cassie to meet as we both checked everybody's schedules so we could all get-together. She kept everyone together to hang out doing summer things like fireworks, summer festivals, fishing tournaments of catching fish and throwing the fish back. We all went to the summer blockbusters together. Cassie arranged a late night test your nerves meet up in a graveyard and at one point; she was able to get us awful sweaty part time jobs so we could all work together. She even brought us back to the batting cages a few times.

After a while, I began to see more than a billion stars and their constellations clearly defined in front of me. Hoshimi sighed and pointed up to a meteor shower cutting across in a moment to light up the night sky in disappearing phosphorescent streaks. Then I felt Cassie gradually slipping her hand into mine. Then she touched my unblemished body, extending beyond the limits of the visible realm. She crossed in undiluted waves of bliss into me with her mind. I felt Penny's hand slowly slide into my other hand. Then I touched her perfect body in an alternate realm with my mind. Both Cassie and Penny turned into me quietly resting their cheek and hand on my chest. A choice to fall in love is better than one to fall apart. An opportunity to live on the breath of the wind is better than a life fixing on the breath of hatred; looking up to the night sky, I see the stars as many as there are and as much as there is on all sides, the silence, and the stars remain black and white.

The Sun They Called the Moon`

Fin...

Epilogue

In the constellation of Sagittarius on the far side of the Milky Way galaxy, an unknown object is sending out radio waves, and the transmission system does not look like anything seen anywhere in the physical universe. The object is located in front of a C.M.E., a coronal mass ejection from a magnetar, a particular type of neutron star. It occurs when a chunk of star sends a magnetic wedge hurling into space, happening when the star squeezes into the size of an asteroid. When a fissure rips across a magnetar's surface and opens, it creates a star quake. A trillion tons of solid matter erupts into deep space with a billion times the magnetic energy of an ordinary star.

The object in the constellation of Sagittarius on the far side of the Milky Way galaxy is generating a magnetic field of its own. It is creating a magnetic umbrella, and funneling trillions upon trillions of energy particles off its wedge, forming a protective umbrella shield, pushing the object like a wind pushing a sail, hurling it through the universe across a million suns at speeds close to light. The object can be detected by the particles of energy coming off the anomaly in an incandescent glow of green for oxygen, blue and red for the nitrogen. These are the colors of the engagement between the magnetic fields, imposing order on chaos. The particles frequently weave their way through the spiral shape galaxies creating invisible waves hundreds of miles across. The object riding on the crest of this particular wave makes the wave visible at the location of the object. The object is sending out radio waves in a rudimentary binary mathematical language to all passersby, if any or to the curious who may be out there, listening, watching if any.

"This is Admiral, Richard Michaels of the Royal Ship, the Argonaut. We are the first human interstellar trans-dimensional travelers and the last hope for our species. Do not intervene; we are in no danger at present. Our Princess, her people, and her crew lay safely in emulator stasis chambers."

The radio waves give up a video signal that reveals a countless number of emulator stasis chambers and focuses on a holographic chart of a small cluster of stars that highlights a third planet and its nearest star. The video signal shows the respiratory activities, faces, and names of the Princess and her crew while in stasis. Some of the names interpreted are as follows:

Penelope Althaea, Princess of the United Federation of Planets,

Richard Michaels, Admiral,

Cassie Jane, Captain,

William Iolaus, First Officer,

Hoshimi Holmes, First Science Officer,

Janie Poeas, First Engineer,

Carolyn Somers, First Doctor,

Greg Tarantino, First Tactical Commander,

Mike Redwood, First Navigator.

Table of Contents

The Sun They Called the Moon`

www.ingramcontent.com/pod-product-compliance
Lightning Source LLC
Chambersburg PA
CBHW030828310726
48980CB00006B/683/J

* 9 7 8 0 5 7 8 1 4 5 7 6 1 *